TRAINING GROUND

An Angel's Epic Adventure to Self-Discovery

Roy M. Dawes Jr

ROY DAWES

PAGE PUBLISHING, INC.
New York, NY

First originally published by Page Publishing, Inc. 2018

ISBN 978-1-64424-706-8 (Paperback)
ISBN 978-1-64424-707-5 (Digital)

Printed in the United States of America

DEDICATION

I would like to dedicate this book to my mother, Lannie. She is the closest thing to an angel on earth I have ever met.

Author: Roy M. Dawes,

I am a thirty-year member of IBEW Local Union 369 in Louisville, Kentucky. I love my career, and I love Kentucky. I am proud to be just a good old boy from Lexington, Kentucky. I love to write. I just wish I could type better. It would sure make writing a book a whole lot easier. For those of you thinking of someday trying to write one, it is an experience I highly recommend. If I can two finger-hit and peck one out, surely, you can too. This is my first book, and I hope it isn't my last. I sincerely hope you all enjoy reading *Training Ground* as much as I enjoyed writing it.

Official Illustrator: Brian Wylie

As you will see inside of this book, Brian Wylie is a very talented artist. Brian owns Custom Creative Services based in Richmond, Kentucky. I am not only fortunate to have Brian on this project as my book's illustrator but hopefully found a lifelong friend. Brian's character and good nature makes him a pleasure to be around.

Custom Creative Services contact information:
Phone: 859-779-4545
E-mail: brian.wylie79@gmail.com

CONTENTS

My Inspiration for Writing This Book

Have you ever wondered why things happen as they do? For instance, I read in the newspaper the other day how an entire carload of family members had been involved in a very horrific accident. Every one of them was killed except one, the mother. It seems the father had even been a preacher—a good man by his friends' accounts that had been written in the local newspaper. Three small kids killed in the wreck were ages two, four, and seven. Why?

This got me thinking. God apparently liked this man and his family, yet they all died except the mother. I couldn't even imagine what she must be going through. Why did he take them? Why did he leave her? God is all-powerful, so he could have prevented the accident in the first place. He could have at least taken all of them. Why did he leave the mother to go through who knows what?

Maybe earth is just one big learning habitat.

But why would God need to teach us something as horrific as what this mother has to endure or the countless other daily sad or equally as bad things that happen? The answer hit me like a slap to the face: angels. It made sense when I thought of this. When God made all the angels, how did he teach such a magnitude of them the things they would need to know to do his will? By that, I mean how to be his heavenly counselors. How do you counsel without experience? How can you fix something you yourself haven't been through? It would make sense that everyone of them needed training, and a lot of it.

They would all need to know life and death, good and evil, winning and losing, and everything else in between that there is to feel. If they were to counsel all of God's future creations, they would need to be experts in emotions. Then they would be ready to do God's will. Maybe earth is one big training ground. Maybe, just maybe, we are the angels, and this is how God is training us. Funny how we all want to go to heaven when we die. Maybe we just want to go home. This is my story.

CHAPTER 1

Angels

Eons ago, God created legions of angels—perfect, beautiful beings who never knew pain, never knew sickness, sorrow, or death. Eternal beings whose only emotion they had ever known was love. Love for each other and love for God, their creator.

The angels lived with God in paradise, in an everlasting heaven filled with a contentment of unconditional love that can only be imagined. Not one wanted anything more than to spend eternity just as it was. But God had plans for them, each and everyone. They were to be his counselors of heaven.

They were to guide, comfort, and be caretakers for all God's future creations. To spread his love and to give hope to the hopeless and peace to the distressed, even to be messengers for God, God knew they would need more than love to do his will. They would need to master all the emotions. They would need to understand the depths of pain and suffering and the thrill of winning to the solace of losing. They would need to know the amazement of birth and the unbearable sorrow of death and to know not just love but hate and, most importantly, faith, compassion, and forgiveness.

So much to teach them and so many, but God, with his infinite wisdom, had it all worked out. He created an amazing blue orb, an entire world full of countless creatures, beautiful landscapes, and everything that would be needed. A perfect training ground he called simply earth, a world where free will along with good and bad decisions would lead them all on endless adventures.

Once in earth, their alter egos would be unknown to them. They would be born and live out entire lives until death, which would bring them back to heaven where they would awaken with all the memories of their time on earth. They would repeat these learning trips for centuries until they had experienced all there was to experience. Then they would be ready, ready to do God's will.

Rarely but occasionally, a small part of the angel's holy spirit would follow that angel being born into earth. And that man or woman, at some point in their lives, sometimes developed some sort of special abilities, super strength, or great wisdom, even ESP or visions. Maybe they are especially kind or stand out in other amazing ways. It happens.

Sometimes God sends angels into the world who have already completed their training to deliver messages and practice their trade on humans in need. Many generations ago, God sent his Son, Jesus, to be born into earth. This was a very big event on earth as it was up in heaven. Unlike angels, Jesus was God's first creation. God made him eons before any of the angels were ever with them.

Like the angels, Jesus used his time on earth to practice his role in setting standards and rules of his fathers—the rules all humans and all future creations of his heavenly father God would have to follow to find everlasting salvation, to fulfill an early covenant that God had set way before at the beginning, and to give a sense of purpose and to offer hope and forgiveness for all angels do as humans while on earth. It not only gave humans hope but also set a bar by which all would be judged, a moral conflict that all would face on a daily basis. His short life on earth taught humans and angels more than any other act ever before or by any other life ever lived.

Before starting, let's shed some light on several things angels as humans go through and why, for example, the reason angels as humans have to sleep when on earth. It seems like such a waste of time since angels never need to sleep when they are in heaven; they just do not require it. Simply put, angels cannot stay away from the Father God Almighty for any lengthy amount of time. That is why without sleep, humans begin to run down and loose clarity. They can become depressed or sometimes even die.

The reason sleep keeps humans vibrant and healthy is that their essence, the Holy Ghost in them, goes back to their heavenly bodies during sleep where it is in the realm of heaven near their Heavenly Father God. That is why when someone is abruptly awaken from sleep or even a nap, humans seem so out of it, so not with their selves. It seems for the first few seconds until they redock and their Holy Spirit returns to them that they are truly not completely with their selves.

Next is dajavue. When angels are lacking in certain training, they are allowed to look over various training guides, showing what may happen in the different lives they may live out. So when they see something as a human that they believe they've seen before, the answer is they probably have seen it; they just hadn't lived it yet.

Let's discuss dreams. Why do humans have them? Dreams are simply a part of the docking process. When going back and forth from earth to heaven, angels always use the same dock, the device used in sending and retrieving angels from earth. It seems it holds all their adventures and memories inside from all the lives they had ever lived out.

Sometimes little outtakes from some of those memories get transferred into the humans' earthly sleeping bodies. So when they have a dream of them falling off a cliff and it seems so real, it scares them almost to death. Chances are, it was real but maybe centuries ago, in some previous life they had lived out. Dreams create fear, wonder, excitement, and speculation about why humans have them in the first place. Humans get training sometimes even when they are asleep and don't know it.

Speaking on that line, let's discuss the arts. There is the theater, television, and the movies, providing constant drama, drama, drama. Some of the first angels God sent down to earth, the ones done with their training, are many times sent to earth to be born to grow up to be actors or singers. Why? Because now while angels are living out one life to learn about emotions and all that go with them. They can watch countless other lives in the process and learn at an expediential rate.

When you hear the catch phrase "He was born to act," believe it. Sadly, this is many times the reason why they cannot stay very long down on earth. They are needed back home in heaven. They come and do God's will and then leave behind them in their huge wake heartbreak, sorrow, love, anger, and, yes, drama. They train humans not only during their lives but also way into their deaths. Elvis's heavenly alter ego was the archangel Michael. J. F. K. was Gabriel. You get the picture.

CHAPTER 2

Tab

This is a story of an angel who was very special to God, a beautiful, very gentle, and kind-spirited angel simply named Tab. Tab had been to earth so many times. She had lived countless lives out on earth, and she could remember every detail of every visit. She loved going to earth. She loved living out all those lives. She loved the adventure and all the drama. Almost as soon as she'd get back to heaven, she'd go back to earth again and again and again.

Her enthusiasm did not go unnoticed. Soon she would be given a great task. She would be given a chance to help earth as no other angel ever had, and God was going to leave it all in her hands as to just what and how she did it—well, almost all in her hands.

A beautiful little girl named Sam was playing hopscotch by herself on her sidewalk joyfully, skipping back and forth. She happily waved to each car as they passed by. It was a perfect day. The sky was so blue, with big, fluffy white clouds that lazily drifted overhead. The strong smell of fresh cut grass lay heavy on the air, and the sounds of summer were everywhere.

A barking dog alerted the little girl to an oncoming red sports car that was speeding down her road. She watched the red car while she continued to skip. Just as the car got to her, the dog, still barking, ran into the path of the car and caused it to swerve right at the little girl. Sam's scream was followed by her mother's scream who witnessed the whole crash from her front porch. The mother was holding the little girl even before the dust cleared.

The mother was sobbing hysterically. "Please, Lord, let her be okay," the little girl's mother prayed out loud. She screamed the little girl's name, "Sam, Sam mommy loves you. Don't die, baby. Momma's here," her mother said, holding her in her arms and sobbing. Sam looked up and tried to speak, but it was too late.

Fade to a well-lit solid white room where a very beautiful, young-looking angelic woman named Tab appeared to be asleep on a floating simple white recliner. Her eyes were closed, and a small tear could be seen as it ran down her cheek. Her eyes abruptly opened, and she gasped, "Mommy, don't cry." Then her facial expression abruptly turned as if she had just come to her senses.

She then stood up from the recliner and dried her eyes. She silently mouthed a little prayer and walked toward a beautiful large door. She paused and looked back toward the chair. The nine years as Sam flooded her thoughts, with all the joy and happiness, her mom and dad, her friends and the little puppy she just got. It still all seemed so real and so vivid.

Her poor mother's face was the last thing she saw as Sam. Her mother was holding her. Crying so hard, she wished she could tell her it was okay, that she was okay. Tab knew full well it was not real, and even with this thought, a tear rolled down her face. She exited the room and entered a colossal coliseum of endless doorways and multiple levels of corridors all filled with rows of doors. Angels could be seen throughout the coliseum on every level as they went in and out of the doorways constantly. It was so big Tab could not even see the end of the coliseum.

As Tab walked home, she greeted every angel that went by. She knew every single one of them on a personal basis. They were all like her brothers and sisters. Tab planned on freshening up when she got home and going straight to see God. She loved telling him of her visits to earth as much as he acted like he loved to hear them. God always made time to see her when she got back from earth.

God was very much like her father as he was to all the angels. They all loved him very deeply, and God loved each and every one of them. Heaven was basically one big family. God was the father, and the angels were all his children, and heaven was their home. That's one reason Tab loved going to earth so much. It was set up just like heaven.

There are parent figures. Humans are just like angels. They work as angels do for God, their Father. They are capable of great things. They just let all the drama get in the way—the greed, jealousy, and sin. It is truly amazing to Tab that humans are angels. Angels are not and could not be capable of such acts.

Humans dream of going to paradise. They all love and want to go to heaven, just like angels do. Most of them naturally love God. They love their families and most try to do the right thing: to help. It just keeps coming back to the drama. But that was God's plan all along. Through the drama is how the angels learn. Tab sometimes get caught up in the theatrics and forget that it's a learning device, a trip to school to teach angels to be able to do God's will properly. But Tab loved it anyway.

Well, Tab is on her way back to the coliseum. She had a really nice visit with God, and as much as she hated to leave him, she was excited about going back to earth. Tab sensed this trip would be like no other, and as strange as it may sound, when Tab told God how excited she was about going back to earth this next time around, she thought she saw him smile for just a split second. But it may have just been her imagination, she thought.

Well, Tab was almost to the coliseum. She always got so excited and nervous just before she would go back to earth. She wondered who she'd be and what she'd say. She wondered what she'd do and what situations she'd face. And as always, once an angel was born into earth, they always forgot who they were. But that was okay with Tab too. She always loved the rush at the end when it all came pouring back at her—that very second she awoke when she could still feel the connection and, at the very moment of clarity, when she knew who she really was. That split second was the best.

Well, here she was at last, back at the coliseum. Tab has lain on this very same dock countless times before. All that was left to do was just lie down and close her eyes and let the adventure begin. Of course, as always, Tab said the same little prayer out loud before she went to earth, "Father, please watch over me and protect me while I am away. Lead and guide my choices while I am on earth. And, God, speed my journey home. Thy will be done on earth as it is in heaven." Tab smiled, let out a small sigh, and then closed her eyes.

"It's a baby girl," said the doctor as he was wrapping the baby up in a warm pink blanket. He handed the baby girl to her father, who in turn, laid her in her mother Christina's arms. Both were teary eyed as they hugged each other and their precious new baby girl. They both were so thankful for this miracle baby.

For seven years, they had tried to have a baby. The countless prayers and tears both Christina and her husband Roy had cried, as each pregnancy test they had taken came back negative. Though Christina had almost given up on ever having a baby, she never lost her faith in God. She knew he had his reasons for everything he did, and her love for him stayed strong.

It seemed like just yesterday when she woke up with those nauseating feelings, and when they kept happening, she remembered the exact moment when it dawned on her. Could she be? Was it possible? Was she pregnant? She recalled how scared she was to ask her husband Roy, to go get yet another pregnancy test. How nervous they both were as they waited and watched as first one then miraculously a second pink line appeared in the test window.

First, silence fell, disbelief, then joy, and then the tears. Both praised God, thanking him from the bottoms of their hearts. That very night just as she was almost asleep, the name Tab came to her. Right then, somehow she knew. She was going to have a little girl, and her name was to be Tab. She also knew in her heart that her new baby girl was a gift from God. And not a day has gone by that she has not thanked him.

Tab was a very happy baby, very alert, and always smiling. As a toddler, she was a joy to be around, so inquisitive, and so cute. She was her mother's joy and her daddy's baby girl. At ten, Tab won her fourth grade spelling bee. At thirteen, she found a little black box lying in the middle of the road. It was full of brand-new diamond rings. She, of course, turned them in. It turned out they were from a local jewelry store.

It seemed a clerk was going to transport them across town and had put them on top of his car to unlock his vehicle since his hands were so full. Being in such a hurry, the clerk forgot to remove them from their perch where they only stayed a few blocks before falling off and into the street where, luckily, they were found by Tab. She had a huge write-up in her town's daily newspaper and even in her school's small newspaper. Her parents were so proud of her as was all her family and friends. As a reward, the jewelry store let her pick out a very nice watch.

At sixteen, Tab was growing into a beautiful young woman—independent, strong-willed, and with a deep love for her parents and for God. Her parents had raised her to know God and his teachings. She never missed church with her parents. She loved reading Bible stories and especially anything to do with angels. Her faith in God was strong; as was this sense that she had always had, she was meant for something big.

On her eighteenth birthday, her parents spent the entire day making it special for her. They made her an angel food cake, her favorite, and ice cream and a huge party for her. So many of her family and friends came to tell her happy birthday! She never felt so loved, never so happy.

What a great day, nothing could top this, she thought! She was going to grab a quick nap after everyone left the party. It was now midafternoon, and later this evening, some of her girlfriends were going to take her shopping and to dinner. A nap would be just what the doctor ordered. She finally said good-bye to her last guest and headed upstairs to her bedroom.

It was fall time, but earlier had been so warm it felt almost like summer outside. But now a cool breeze was coming in through her window, perfect napping weather. She lay down on her bed and closed her eyes. Tab yawned and stretched out her arms, opened her sleepy eyes from her nap, and gasped! Two huge thoughts rushed at her.—one, *Why is it dark?* And two, *Why am I back in heaven?*

CHAPTER 3

The Awakening

I wasn't even sick back on earth. Something was not right, and Tab knew it. Heaven is never dark, never. Just then, she heard a distant dog barking, and this really freaked her out. There are no dogs in heaven. *Oh my, I am still on earth! I am still in my bedroom!*

Tab now realized the obvious truth that she had awakened from her nap to have full knowledge of her angelic self. She immediately jumped out of her bed and flipped on the light switch. Tab turned to the mirror on her dresser, and in total disbelief, she was staring at a perfect reflection of what she looked like in heaven. Minus her wings. Even her name Tab was the same.

One huge difference now crept at her very quickly. She did not feel her Heavenly Father's inner connection she had always had with him. Since her creation, Tab had felt God's presence as though he was standing right beside her no matter where she traveled, with or without him. Everywhere but on her trips to earth, that is.

Tab was saddened by this, scared even. She had never been alone. She did know one thing. Whatever was happening, her Heavenly Father God was behind it. Nothing happened without him knowing about it. But what did he want her to do? What was his purpose? To the best of her knowledge, no one but Jesus had ever been born unto earth and learned of their heavenly preexistence.

Wow, now there was something truly deep to think about, Tab thought. His life on earth was the most important life ever lived. She knew firsthand all Jesus went through and all he accomplished with his time down here on earth. Tab had been a young water girl named Olivia during his time on earth.

Tab stopped and remembered. She remembered vividly standing in the market the day a huge uproar came toward her:

Like everyone else, I ran to see what was going on. A mob of people had followed some soldiers who were screaming and yelling, and I fought my way through the crowd to get a better look.

There dragging this huge wooden cross was this bloody, bruised, half-beaten-to-death man named Jesus. They stopped briefly right in front of me as the soldiers tried to clear a path down the road as people were gathering from all directions to see what was happening. The man went to one knee under the strain of the weight of the large wooden cross.

Though scared, the soldiers would punish me if they saw me. I stepped out of the crowd and knelt beside him. His lips were so parched looking as I dipped my ladle into the cool water and brought it to his lips. He was so bloody, so beat his eyes were swelled almost completely shut. Someone had made a crown of thorns and pushed it so hard down upon his head that blood came out from around several of the thorns.

I couldn't help myself, and I started crying as he sipped the cool water. And with all he was going through, he raised his head and looked straight into my eyes and said, "Cry not for me, Olivia, and cast your prayers out not on my behalf but on the fears of men. For today, our Father God Almighty will open a path to everlasting salvation. A promise that with my death, my sacrifice, all who believe in me and accept me as their Savior may live forever. Go spread these words and tell all who have faith that death is no longer something they need to fear."

The whip made a thunderous crack as the soldier brought it against his bloody back. I fell back, spilling my water from the surprise attack. Looking up, I saw Jesus trying to stand, pain still on his face from the whip. A brave and good man from the crowd stepped out and helped lift the huge wooden cross up so Jesus could get back on his feet.

He looked again at me and saw the fear and shock on my face. He nodded at me as if to say, 'It's okay. God is with me." And he continued on his way. The way he had been beaten, I remembered wondering how he could even stand. But there he went, dragging this huge wooden cross. I will never forget that day.

Even now centuries later as Tab reflected back on that day, a large tear rolled down her face.

Tab thought to herself, *God and I have never spoken of that day. But the angels and I sure have. We all know the earthly reason why he sent Jesus: to set standards in the way humans and all other future creations of his should live, love, and honor one another and God. That by faith and accepting Jesus Christ as their Savior, all may find a pathway to heaven.*

Because all of us angels know that this earth is only a practice world, a training ground, we all know that no matter what we do while on earth, we will still come back to heaven—it is our home. God even promised all of us angels in the very way he named earth: Every Angel Returns To Heaven. So all of the angels and I agree that we think God did it because of all we, as angels, have had to endure on earth in our training missions.

The pain, the sickness and loss, the heartbreak, and suffering that we all go through, is for him so we all will be able to do his will to his standards. God never makes any of us go. We all go because we love him, and we all want to make him happy. God knows this and the other angels, and I believe he endured the pain and tribulation of watching his firstborn Jesus go through all that he went through. It was his way to show all of the angels he is in this with us.

It not only changed earth but heaven as well. All us angels know how Jesus was treated. It hurt our Father. What Father would ever want to see his son go through such torture and be sacrificed? No Father could love you more than one willing to go through what he endured. And he did it all for us. To show just how much he loved all of us angels. What a Father!

Tab was almost to the point of fainting with all the thoughts that rushed to her. She needed her Father now more than ever, his guidance and his assurance. Whatever his reasons were, she knew this was an honor, a gift. She closed her eyes and prayed for guidance. And even though she had no answers, she had known her Heavenly Father God long enough to know he had them. She was sure things would work out and that her path would be shown to her. She started calming down as that thought started really sinking in.

Now that she was calming down, she started wondering what all she may be able to do. As a human, angels have all their emotions but usually no special powers. But normally, angels can do so many amazing things in the name of the father. Sometimes they can heal, and having thought this, she looked down at her arm where a very small scratch just happened to be. Tab put her hand on it, closed her eyes, and said a little prayer. She removed her hand and was disheartened that the scratch was still there.

What else could she try? Tab stopped and silently thought for a moment. "Oh yeah, I can close my eyes and picture myself to be anywhere I want to be. So here goes," Tab said almost in a whisper. She closed her eyes and said a little prayer and then pictured herself sitting next to her Heavenly Father God. Tab smiled big in the hope that when she opened her eyes that she would indeed be sitting next to him. She said her little prayer, the same one she always did when she moved around using the Holy Spirit.

Tab slowly opened her eyes and presto. Sadly, she was still sitting on her bed alone. *That didn't work either*, she thought to herself. "Looks like all I have is my memory, and I don't know how that will help," Tab spoke out loud. "Father, what am I to do without the heavenly powers you allow me to use when I do your will? Could I not best serve you as like when I am in heaven? As an eighteen-year-old human, Father, I am afraid of failing you."

Tab spent several minutes feeling sorry for herself before realizing that her Father loved her. He would surely not set her up for failure. Now she felt ashamed for her lack of faith. Once again, she spoke out loud to her Heavenly father, "Dear Heavenly Father, forgive my shortcomings. I will not fail you. I know you are with me as you have always been. You are my strength and the only power I will ever need. Please show me the path you wish me to take. I am your servant, and I will do your will as best as I am able as I always do in heaven."

Tab looked down at her watch. She had less than an hour to get ready before her friends got there, and she wondered if she should even go now. She knew her Heavenly Father God put her here in this life for a reason. So her instincts told her to just go and see what happened.

Back at home now finally, and boy, was she tired. Tab's friends went all out to show her a great time, and she was so glad she went. She went through her house until she found her parents. Before Tab told her parents good night, she began telling them about her wonderful evening with her girlfriends. When she was finished, she hugged them both and told them good night. The television in the background displayed an unnoticed breaking news story.

CHAPTER 4

The Affliction

It's morning here on earth, and what am I supposed to do? Tab thought to herself as she rubbed her sleepy eyes. She smelled breakfast but no way could she eat. She wondered why her mother had not called her down though, a strange but welcomed event. Tab sat up and closed her eyes, and you could just see the concentration on her face.

She began to silently pray, "Why can't I feel you with me, Father? I have never been alone before. Please show me what I am to do so I can come home." She opened her eyes and rubbed them one more time. She got up, threw some clothes on, and headed down stairs.

Tab's mother had food on the table, but she was not in the kitchen. She hollered for both her mother and her father, but neither one answered her. She heard the television and headed into the living room. There sat both her parents with her aunt Marilyn and uncle Larry. Tab loved it when they came over for a visit.

"Hey everybody, you guys didn't hear me? I've been yelling for you," Tab asked everyone. Even as she stood in the same room with everyone, no one answered her. All four of them, she now noticed, were intensely watching the television set.

"Honey, sit down," her mother whispered, patting the couch beside her. Tab did as her mother asked her. The television was showing yet another breaking news story. The local news anchorman Dan Allen was in Northern Angola standing by what looked like a large group of African tribesmen. He turned toward the camera. "Ladies and gentleman, viewing what I am about to show you is very graphic and very disturbing," the anchorman said. A video started playing on the television screen. The anchors voice continued, "This was shot yesterday morning from Lacasa, in Northern Angola. Lacasa is a small mining village.

"News of what you are about to see aired last night on our evening news program. This video was sent to us after our broadcast went off the air. This video showed the situation to be much graver than first suspected. Our field reporter Brady Bair and Rodney, the cameraman who shot this video along with all of their crew, have not been heard from since sending out this video. Everyone here at NBS fear the worse," the anchorman sadly said.

The video appeared to show the complete desolation of the entire village. The video panned back and forth as it traveled down the center of the village. On the video, people were dead everywhere, including men, women, and children. Even livestock and dogs were shown dead. Apparently, even the animals were not immune to whatever was responsible for killing the people.

The camera briefly stopped on a close-up of a woman's face who was lying dead right in the middle of the road. There were little blue boils all over her, and the boils had tiny, squiggly lines that ran out from the center of each one. The video ended as Tab sat back on the couch and brought her knees up to her face. The television camera panned back to the anchor who continued his coverage.

"It seemed one lone miner by the name of CJ Martin came out of the mines yesterday morning covered in these little blue boils. Now it is very apparent that whatever it was that killed this poor unfortunate miner and made him break out with the blue boils was also responsible for rapidly spreading throughout this small Northern Angolan village and killing everyone it came into contact with. As of this moment, authorities say there has been no further communications from the village or even the surrounding areas. Our prayers go out to all of these villagers and to all of our missing crew members and their families.

"Since this video was first seen, authorities have quarantined the area, and all travel in and out of the area have been banned. Top medical expert Jim Pyron in the field of pathology, just earlier in a press conference, said nothing like these blue boils have ever been seen before. Top government officials along with Keith Roach, the United States diplomat to Angola, have said that until we know what we are dealing with that quarantining the area is our only defense. The Angolan government and the United States government along with the UN Council have all agreed to put their very best medical personnel to work on figuring this out. They hope to find out what they are dealing with and to stop its spread. We will keep you updated as we learn more," the anchorman smiled as he went off the air. The oldest of the tribesmen who stood next to the anchor said something in Umbundo just as the broadcast went off the air. Tab sat straight up and then stood up. Tab then abruptly sat back down and put her hands over her face.

"Tab, are you okay?" her father asked.

"What the old man said might be right. He said it might be the end of us all," Tab answered.

"No one said that. what are you talking about?" Tab's mother asked her.

"The old tribesmen said it," Tab replied, pointing her finger at the television where the old man had just been.

"Honey, unless you can speak African, which I do not remember you learning, why do you think he said that?" her mother asked, puzzled.

"Mom, he wasn't speaking African. He was speaking Umbundo. A really old form of it too, and that is what he said," Tab said as she stood up. Tab turned and gave her aunt and uncle a big hug and politely said good-bye to them. She looked at her father. "Dad, can you please come with me? I need to talk to you," Tab asked her father, Roy.

Her father followed her into the next room. Tab turned to her father and, with tears in her eyes, told him. "Dad, I know you will have trouble believing what I am about to tell you. Mostly because I can't fully tell you how I know everything I know. But you know I never lie to you or mom. And I promise everything I am about to tell you is true.

19

"I have seen this outbreak before. These blue boils are bad, Dad, really bad. They are totally lethal when they start spreading. They have killed off entire continents before. But I think—" Tab said as she was suddenly interrupted by her father.

"Tab, you're talking crazy, entire continents. Honey, this thing is new. You heard what the experts on the television said, honey? Nobody has ever seen this before. Why are you talking this way, Tab? You're not making any sense." Her father told her.

Tab looked her father right in the eyes. "Because it's true. I have seen this before, Dad. I think I can stop this. I believe I was put here to stop this. But I need you to believe in me and trust me—maybe even help me," Tab told her father.

"Tab, I don't understand. Help you how? What do you want me to believe? How in the world do you know about this?" her father questioned.

An idea occurred to Tab. "Dad, you know me better than anyone—even better than mom does. Yes or no? Do I know any other languages," Tab asked her father.

"No, none that I know of," her dad replied.

Tab, knowing her father could speak several languages fluently, then said. "Dad, if I can converse with you in any language you can throw at me, even any you want to look up—if I can do that, will you not ask any questions about how I know what I know even though that will in itself create so many other questions? Please say you will, Dad. I really need you to have faith in me. I am going to need your help to even have a chance at stopping this," Tab pleaded with her father.

Her father looked at the sincerity in his little girl's face. And not seeing how he could lose this little test looked Tab dead in her eyes. "Yes, Tab, I will help you." Her father smugly said in a Tahitian dialect.

"Do you promise me, Dad," Tab replied back in the same Tahitian dialect.

"Why, of course, I will promise you?" her father answered her back in Ingush, a Russian dialect.

"Then please do, my father. I need to hear you say the words," Tab replied back perfectly in the Russian dialect of Ingush. This second answer made her father pause, and he even took a step back. Shocked but determined to somehow end this insanity, her father regrouped and started asking random questions in every language he knew. Tab answered every one to his amazement in perfect dialect.

Her father then stood up but told her to stay put. He went to his den and carried back with him several books on other languages he had been trying to learn. He started systematically going through each book and asked her the meaning of words he was trying to sound out. Once again, Tab not only knew every word and its meaning, but she even started helping her father pronounce some of the words correctly. Her father's head dropped, and he looked so dazed he looked almost sick.

With a beaten, lost look on his face, he raised his head and simply said, "I promise. What do we need to do? How can I help you stop this, baby girl," asked her father. Tab came over and hugged her dad tightly. She knew he was tore up and confused right now, but she knew she would need his help if she was to have any chance of stopping this affliction. After all, she was only eighteen years old.

"Thank you Daddy, but I am not exactly 100 percent sure on the plan yet. Will you tell Mom I need to be alone for a little while? I need to work on all this," Tab whispered in Spanish to her father.

Dad just shook his head and said, "Si."

Tab went to her bedroom and closed the door. She kneeled down at the foot of the bed and started talking to God. She talked and talked for well over an hour before she finally got up. Though he never answered her back, she knew he heard every word.

Tab stood up and sat up on the bed. She then slid up until her back was against the headboard, and she closed her eyes. Tab started remembering every time she had ever encountered this affliction, this outbreak. The only way she knew to fight this was to try and remember details that she did not know were important. Something she missed in one of her past lives.

Something had to be there. Something she saw or heard that at the time might not have seemed important but now held the key to fighting this thing. Tab let her angelic, perfect memory whisk her away deep into her past, clear back to when she first encountered these blue boils, centuries back.

Meanwhile back downstairs, her father was being questioned by her mother. Tab's aunt Marilyn and uncle Larry had said their good-byes and left, and now Mom wanted to know what was going on. All her father knew to tell her was that something—something amazing—had come into their daughter.

"Come into her? What are you saying, Roy?" her mother Christina, asked.

"I'm not sure what I am saying really. Just that she's changed somehow, she knows things, things she shouldn't possibly know," her father Roy replied.

Suddenly, her mother dropped to her knees. "It's got to be God. She's always been my little miracle, and now maybe she's Gods," her mother told her father.

Tab's father hugged her mother tightly. "That's as good a guess as any baby. It just may be God working in her," her father whispered. Meanwhile upstairs, Tab was still sitting on her bed. But her mind was centuries away. *The year was 351 BC,* Tab remembered.

CHAPTER 5

Past Lives

It was in the fall of that year that I first encountered the blue boils. It was just starting to get good and cold. I was only seventeen but already a mother of three. My babies' names were Jordan, Mika, and Jasmine, and my name was Elizabeth Scott during this life. I was married and my husband's name was Stacy. He was seventeen also. Seventeen was considered to be a man back in those days.

Stacy was a good man. He always provided for the children and me. We were so in love with each other. I cherished the ground he walked on. We were farmers and shepherds and had been blessed to build up quite a nice herd of goats. We lived on the outskirts of a very small village just a day's walk from Mandonesia. Mandonesia was the thriving metropolis of its time.

Stacy and I depended on each other for everything, and although we both worked very hard every day, we were happy and content with our lives. Times were a lot tougher than they are now. If you didn't work hard everyday, you simply did not survive back in those times. Working hard was just a normal thing everyone did back then.

We were tending our goats in one of our fields when our closest neighbors, Ray and his wife, Becky, walked up with their newborn daughter, Ryan. Ray was trying to explain about an affliction he had heard about happening in Mortinea, a village just west of Mandonesia. Three days later, Mandonesia was desolated. One day after that, a sickly man walked into our village broke out with little blue boils.

We did all we could do for the poor, sickly man. We knew nothing of germs back then. A few hours later, he was dead. One day later, my village, my family, and I all died.

Tab was a little saddened by this memory. Tab wiped away a tear and continued on, *The year was 17 AD. It was fall time again, the second time I encountered the blue boils. It was a beautiful day, much warmer than usual for that time of year. Just the day before had been freezing, so this was a very welcome surprise.*

I was a fourteen-year-old girl named Talia. I had three sisters, Val, Raylie, and Shaylie and two little brothers, Quinton and Braden. Families had a lot of children back then to help tend the fields. My family and I were traveling with our village. We were all in search of a new settlement, a place we could call home. We needed a more fertile area to relocate to.

I loved where our old village was, but my father, Duke, said our water was going dry and that the men had hunted all the animals until there was no more to hunt—that if the village didn't move, we would not be able to survive the coming winter. We had all been traveling for weeks trying to find a new home. My family was traveling near the front of the convoy when talk of a settlement had been seen up ahead.

The entire convoy stopped until our leaders could decide on a course of action. Finding a village way out in the middle of nowhere only held a 50 percent chance that good people ran it. It certainly paid to be wary of that other 50 percent. It certainly did not mean we had found sanctuary or even safe passage around it.

My father and several others left to go try and speak with them. Times were very dangerous back then, so the rest of us stayed hidden until they returned. They were only gone a very short time before they returned. I could hear the fear in their voices when they explained what they had seen.

My father, Duke, said everyone in the village was dead. That everyone was covered in little blue boils. The convoy took a very wide path around that village, and we traveled on. Several of the men including my father went back and burned all the bodies and the village itself. Looking back now, it seemed strange that we never caught it as contagious as it seemed to be. Why didn't it spread to us? Tab thought.

A knock at her bedroom door abruptly brought Tab back. "Come in," she answered.

Her father Roy, walked in and sat on her bed with her and grabbed her hand and held it. "What do we need to do?" her father asked her.

"Dad, I still need some more time. Then if you're okay with it, I want to tell you some stories and see if you can help me find something in them, something that I keep missing that might help beat this thing," Tab replied.

Dad looked a bit confused. "Stories, Tab, what kind of stories? How can stories help stop this?" her father asked.

Tab said in Spanish, "Dad please, I promise to explain as much as I can but only later. Now I have to get back to what I was doing. I need to concentrate so I don't miss anything. I will be done soon and I will come down and get with you in just a little while," Tab told him.

Tab's father looked a little more assured hearing Tab speak Spanish. Roy nodded his head, but as he got up to head to the door, he turned. "Tab, your mother," her father Roy said as Tab interrupted him.

Tab had sensed her father's dilemma. "Dad, just bring Mom with you. We may need all the help we can get," Tab told him. Dad sighed with relief and closed the door as he walked out. Tab took her place back on her bed and closed her eyes again. She resumed thinking about all the times she had been to school and all the lives she had ever lived. Especially the lives with the little blue boils in them. Tab knew the answer was in there somewhere—she just had to find it. Tab said a silent little prayer and prayed for help and guidance from her Heavenly Father God Almighty.

Tab's mind once again whisked her all the way back to the year 683 AD: *It was summertime and as hot as it had ever been. I was an old woman when I first seen the blue boils in this life. My name was Lannie, but everybody called me Grandma Lannie.*

I lived in an old mining village with my family under a big mountain. I had seven children, three sons and four daughters, and some twenty-six grandchildren. All the men in the village, including my three sons, mined bronze out of our big mountain. Our king, King William, paid the men of our village well for the bronze they mined. He gave each of them land and livestock for their hard work. Mining was a very dangerous profession, and King William knew it. He needed the bronze, and he didn't mind paying our people to get it.

I was holding one of my twenty-six grandbabies when my eldest son John, and three of his miner friends, Dewey, Glen and Edward, brought in my brother Wayne. He was just seven years younger than I was. The men said he had been gone a long time in the caves alone when they finally saw him come stumbling out of the mine. They said he collapsed as they walked toward him. Wayne had broken out all over in little blue boils.

By late afternoon, Wayne had died. We burned his body that very night. The men said he had gone into a new area of the mine. One recently opened up when new tunnels were created by rumbles—earthquakes as they are called now. He had gone looking for new pockets of bronze.

That area of new tunnels was permanently closed off after Wayne's death. The men were all too afraid to go in there, afraid they too would catch the blue boils. They said it was cursed, and we all believed it. No other incidents with the blue boils ever reoccurred while I lived in the village until my death.

Once again, why did it not spread to any of us? This is making no sense. This may be a waste of time, Tab thought to herself. But knowing her memory was all she had to work with, she knew she must continue.

The last time before today that I had an encounter with this affliction was in the year 1349. I lived on the now-infamous island of Atlantis. I was royalty then. My name was Princess Loraleigh. I was the king's niece, my mother, Princess Sherry, was the king's sister.

The king, King Hearl, and his beautiful wife Queen Lorene, loved my mother and I. The king was a good man, and all the people he ruled loved their king. I was sixteen and very happy with my life on the island. Atlantis was a wondrous place to live. My uncle Prince Phillip and I rode our white stallions nearly every day up and down the beautiful beaches of our island. Every day was like a gift.

It's amazing to me how fast things can turn. It all started on a day that was supposed to be a day of rejoicing. For that day, a trader's ship was scheduled to come bringing us much-needed supplies. King Hearl always had mother and me a present or two on board. The both of us always looked forward to those ships showing up. But today, it had not shown up yet. We feared the weather might be the reason for it running late. The weather had been so perfect as of late, but the last couple of days had been bitter cold, way too cold for such an island paradise.

Finally, there was news that the ship had arrived. The king himself went to the docks to see what had taken so long. He also liked talking with the captains and hearing their stories they always told. This captain the king knew well. He called him Skipper.

Skipper was a lifelong man of the sea. He had been on ships his whole life. He had been everywhere, and we all loved it when he told stories of his adventures. Skipper was from our nearest neighbor, Sandora, on the mainland just several hours off our coast.

My mother Sherry, and I went to the docks with the king. We wanted our presents we knew would be on board. Maybe we would not have gone if we had known what else the ship had brought with it. The king asked Skipper why he had ran so late. The captain explained that he had trouble getting enough help loading his ship—that an illness had broken out on Sandora and that people were too busy tending to their sick. The captain said that a few of the men he had hired to help load his ship were telling stories of deadly blue boils infecting people, covering their bodies and eventually killing them.

The captain told our king he was glad to be out of there. King Hearl immediately looked concerned and asked the captain about the health of his crew members. The captain who had just started to cough tried to assure the king that every one of his crew members was strong and healthy. The captain and all his crew members were dead within several hours.

The affliction as it was called back then spread fast and killed fast. It only took about fourteen hours until those of us at the docks had come down with symptoms, a few hours more when the blue boils came upon us. About five hours after the blue boils broke out on someone, they would be dead.

Within four days, my entire island had been wiped out. My king, mother, and I were all dead. Two months later, the entire island sank into the Pacific Ocean when the volcano that made it suddenly blew up. No one knows this, but by then, it was just a deserted, sad little island, Tab thought as she remembered all she knew to remember.

It was late now. Tab had spent the entire day and evening reliving her past. She went downstairs to see her parents. She told them she was ready but that as late as it was that the morning might be a better time to start.

"Tab, start what?" her mother Christina, asked.

Tab went over to hug her mother. She could sense her concern. As Tab and her mother held each other tightly, Tab felt her mother's tension slowly melting away. "Tomorrow, Mom. You and Dad get some sleep. I will need you both fresh for tomorrow," Tab told her mother. Tab felt her mother nod her head as she continued holding her.

She wished she could just tell them that if it all went real bad that the worst thing that would happen is they all would just get to go home. Go back to heaven and be with their Heavenly Father God. But she sensed he would not want them to know that. Tab believed that God wanted her to figure this out, save as many lives as possible, and spread his word. Tab told both of her parents good night, and then she went upstairs.

It wasn't that late, but Tab was worn completely out. Tab knew she was an angel, but she sure didn't feel like one. In heaven, she, along with all the other angels, never have to sleep. They just do not require it. Now it's all she can think about. Well, that and not having her connection with God. To her, that was the hardest part of this mission, this test, or whatever it was. She said her prayers and told God how much she loved and missed him, and then she went to sleep.

It's morning time, and Tab rolled over and rubbed her sleepy eyes. "Good morning Father. I pray you're with me today. I have a feeling I will need your help more than anybody's," Tab said softly. Tab quickly showered, got dressed, and headed downstairs.

Her mom and dad were already sitting at the kitchen table drinking coffee. They loved their coffee in the mornings. Her mother had her a plate of food sitting on the table, along with a small glass of orange juice. No one talked other than quick good mornings.

Tab ate. She was so hungry. She got so into her past last night she never came down for dinner. Mom and Tab put away the breakfast wares. Dad was busy pouring him and her mother another cup of coffee. After everything was cleared off the table and put away, Tab motioned for everyone to follow her into the living room. This could take a while, and she thought everyone should be comfortable.

In the living room, everyone took their normal place and sat down. Tab looked right at both of her parents, and she could see how nervous and tense they were. Both of her parents stared back at her waiting for who knew what. Tab stood and paced for a moment.

Her dilemma was how to tell them everything they needed to know to help her without telling them everything. The truth or at least a good half-truth seemed to be the only answer she came up with.

CHAPTER 6

Brainstorming

"Mom and Dad," Tab said, "without lying to you, which you two know I never do, I will tell you both up front that I cannot tell you everything you are going to want to know. But everything I do tell you will be the truth as unbelievable as it is going to sound. So here goes, and I hope you both keep an open mind. I need you both to believe every word I am about to tell you," Tab hopefully told her parents.

"I know things about this outbreak, these blue boils, a lot of things. How I know is what I do not want to share with you. I just think it would hurt more than help," their daughter told them.

"Okay Tab, we both agree," her father said, and her mother nodded her head yes in agreement. "What do you need us to do?" her father continued.

"Tab, it has spread more. It's all the news is talking about," her mother interrupted.

"I was afraid that was going to happen. When this stuff spreads, it spreads fast. But sometimes it doesn't spread at all. Sometimes you can even touch it and nothing happens. How can something so contagious one minute be so uncatchable the next? I believe if we can figure the answer out to that question, we will be on our way to stopping this.

"I know the answer is in the stories I am getting ready to tell you both. I just need help finding it. I just cannot put my finger on the answer. Next, we have to try to convince people we are not crazy and get them to try whatever we come up with," Tab told them both.

"We will cross that bridge when we come to it. Let's find a way to stop this first. So what have you got for us baby girl, tell us?" her father asked.

"Wait a minute and let me write this all down so we can go over it later," her mother told Tab.

"It's a lot, mom," Tab said.

"It's what I do," Tab's mother replied. Christina was a stenographer at their local courthouse.

So Tab started telling tale after tale to her parents. Tab could sense how bad they wanted to ask her how she knew all what she was telling them. They stopped for lunch, and once again no one spoke, but everyone was thinking about all the stories they had just listened to, thinking about how this or that connected to each story they had just heard.

After lunch, Tab went right back into telling her stories. Mom was still writing it all down. Dad had even been making his own notes. Finally, at about eight in the evening, Tab finished her last story. Tab looked up. "That's all I know. I got nothing else," Tab told them.

Her father Roy, stood up and looked at her mom and asked her to please go make everyone a copy of her manuscript and of his notes. Dad then turned to Tab. "Amazing stuff. You sure you didn't just dream all of this?" asked her father. Tab shook her head no as her father shook his head no in unison with Tab's as if he had already knew what her answer was going to be.

"Well, okay then. I have a few thoughts already, but let's split up when your mother returns, and we'll spend what's left of tonight each going over all of this alone. Then in the morning, we will meet back down here and brainstorm together," her father told Tab. Tab's mother Christina, walked back in after she had copied everything, and she just could not help herself.

"Tab, the way you told those stories, you've seen all of this, haven't you?" Tab's mother asked. Tab looked at the intensity in her mother's eyes and simply shook her head yes. A tear rolled down her mother's face, and she knew right there and then that this all laid at the feet of the Almighty himself, God. Tab hugged her mother and held her tightly. Tab's mom was crying, but Tab sensed they were tears of joy.

After a long and restless night, the three of them were back at the breakfast table once again. Only this time unlike before, all three of them were talking a hundred miles an hour. Each seemingly having caught something different from the stories Tab had told the night before.

Tab's father cleared his voice and did his best fake cough. "Okay girls, let's go one at a time. Who wants to go first?" he asked.

Both Tab and her mother at the same time said, "Go ahead." Then each mocked his fake cough.

Dad smiled, and the girls laughed. "Here is what I came up with. It isn't much, but here goes. From what you said, it seems to me that every time the blue boils spread, the temperature was cool to cold. Every time it did not spread, it was hot or, as you said Tab, unusually warm. Also, it is safe to assume that it comes from the ground since twice it was contracted by miners, and caves stay at a pretty much constant temperature of about fifty-eight degrees. I'm guessing, but fifty-eight degrees to a tropical island would probably feel like it was bitter cold," Tab's father told them both.

"Wow Dad, that was a good catch," Tab told her father.

Mom jumped in the conversation. "I think I got something, and it's terrifying actually, but every date you gave us when these outbreaks occurred, even yesterday's, they are all exactly 666 years apart," her mother said with fear in her eyes.

Both Tab and her father sat straight up. "Wow, that is terrifying," Tab's father said.

"What does that mean? Why is it exactly 666 years between outbreaks? I am scared you guy's is this the end of everything?" Tab's mother, asked. Both her mother and her father looked at Tab like she held the answer to that question.

Tab said the only thing she knew to say, "If it is God's will Mom and Dad, then so be it. Remember we are Christians and we have all three been saved and baptized. If this all goes bad, I know where I am going, and you should too." Tab wished she could just confirm this truth, but she felt her Heavenly Father would want them to do this on faith. "I feel it is important to tell you both that I do not believe that this is the end. I believe I was put here for a reason, maybe to stop this affliction," Tab said. Both her parents felt a little better after hearing Tab's little speech.

The phone rang and interrupted their conversation. It was Tab's uncle Larry, and he told Roy to quickly turn on the television and watch the morning news channel. Uncle Larry told Tab's dad to hurry so he wouldn't miss what was on.

CHAPTER 7

The Spread

Dad hung up and went over to the television set and turned it on. First thing on the news was the president of the United States being interviewed about the outbreak. President Richard Worsham talked about how fast it had spread throughout Northern Angola, how contagious it was, and how hard it seemed to be able to contain.

He then switched to another of his agendas and tried to tie the two together. The president was a very religious man, and everyone knew it. Since his election, the president had been all about trying to get prayer back into the schools. Always saying how much better the world and the United States was before the Ten Commandments had been removed from every courthouse and school wall throughout this great land of ours.

He said two huge differences now existed since the days when he went through the public school system back in the times of school prayer and religious Christmas plays and such. The first thing was prayer and the Ten Commandments had been removed from the schools and courthouse walls. And second, kids now came to school on a regular basis and shot the place and themselves up. Schoolchildren of all ages commonly disrespect their teachers, their parents, and their selves.

The president said how obvious it was that the two differences had to be clearly connected. And that if we did not get back to the way it was, back when "We the people' put God first and held up his teachings everywhere that we had a wall to hang them on, this country was heading down a road they may not be able to come back from. He also said that prayer anytime and every time was always and forever a great thing to do no matter where it was done. He boldly said that with an event like the one happening in Angola that God and prayer may be the only answer there was.

"That's why he got our vote," Tab's father said out loud, talking about his and his wife's vote. As soon as the president was finished with his interview and went off, the local news anchor once again began talking about the outbreak in Northern Angola. He said the news station of the missing reporter theorized that the missing reporter and his crew must had drove to the next little village outside the quarantined area before succumbing to the infection.

There they must have accidentally infected others, and with so many little villages so close together, it spread like a wildfire. The UN had since quarantined all of Angola. Probably the most interesting thing all three of them heard was when one of the many anchors talking throughout the broadcast had said how unseasonably cool it had been for this time of year in Angola. The anchor said the last few days had set records in Angola and that the temperature had barely gotten over fifty-five degrees.

Dad shut the television off, and instantly, the three of them knew they were on to something. Tab started talking, almost feverishly.

"Dad, you may be right. Maybe that is it. Maybe that's why it never spread to me or my other families. It was warm both times it never spread. Maybe the heat does kill it, or at least shuts it down, maybe heat is the antidote," Tab excitedly said without thinking.

Her mother and her father looked at each other at the same time. "Your other families," they both said out loud.

"Why, you never caught it. Tab, did you have visions of this? Your father and I were thinking you must have been shown visions of all of this. Or are you saying these stories"—she paused—"you told us, are about you?" her mother asked.

Tab knew she slipped up and thought of the one out, the one truth she knew they would believe. "God is the answer to all of this. He is pretty much the answer to any and all your questions about any of this," Tab told her mother and her father. They both were intently looking at her as she continued, "I am your daughter, but I have been"—Tab paused and searched for the right word—"enlightened. I have been daughters to many other families as well. I am a very old soul to say the least," Tab tried to explain.

"Is this why you know so many languages?" her father asked her.

"Actually Dad, I can speak every language ever spoken since time on this earth began," Tab answered her father, not thinking about just how brutally honest and how telling her answer really was.

Her father and mother looked at each other and mouthed, "Since time began."

Her father tried to lighten the moment. "Well, I always wanted you to learn another language. I guess I got my wish," her father joked as Tab and him shared a half laugh. Tab's mother was still trying to come to grips with what Tab had told them.

Tab looked at her mother. "Mom, are you okay?" Tab asked.

"Yeah, I'm good," her mother replied as she stared straight ahead.

Dad tried again to lighten the mood. "Good, honey our baby girl is going to save the world. We're great. We are kind of like Mary and Joseph." Her father told her mother in an attempt to pick her spirits up.

"Dad, that may be a little much," Tab replied to her father about his comment. But what her father Roy had said, somehow struck a chord inside of her mother, and Christina perked right up.

"No Tab, your father may be right. You're still our daughter even you said you were. We are like Mary and Joseph. My baby's going to save the world," her mother Christina excitedly said out loud. Tab looked over at her dad who was smiling.

"See what you started dad? Wow guys, bring it down a notch. I haven't saved anything yet," Tab told her parents. *At least they were both smiling now, that went better than expected*, Tab thought.

"Maybe not, but we are on to something. I am convinced that heat plays a role in how it spreads. Since it lives in the cool underground, heat may shut it down, maybe even kill it. It's about all we got," Tab's father said.

"How do we use this information? Who do we know that could use this information to fight this thing?" Tab asked.

"Leave that to your dad. He knows who to call. It's kind of what he did back before you were born," her mother replied.

"Since we are all being so honest here, I guess I will too. I'm an ex-CIA agent, baby girl. I quit when you were born. It's why Daddy knows so many different languages," her father told her.

"I guess, if you think seven different languages is so many," laughed Tab, joking back at her father.

"Ha-ha, very funny, Miss Knows-Every-Language-Since-Time-Began," her dad said, chuckling.

"She's got your sense of humor, Roy. She is still our baby girl," her mother chimed in.

"Of course I am you two," Tab declared. "Who are you going to call, Dad?" Tab asked, looking concerned. "What are you going to tell them?" she continued.

"Pretty sure I know who to call. Getting him not to hang up on me is what I don't know. I need everyone's input on this. How do I convince my friend to believe me? How are we supposed to know so much about this—about something no one ever supposedly even seen or heard about before?" her father asked both his wife and Tab.

"Do you think if we went in person I could convince them? Do you think my knowing so many languages would work like it did with you?" Tab asked her father.

"No Tab," her father quickly responded. "These are not the kind of people you want to show off in front of. They would want to keep you," her father continued.

Tab looked at her dad and put her hand on his shoulder and softly said, "What other choice do we have? People are dying, a lot of people. If this spreads much farther, we may not even be able to stop it. Maybe they will just offer me a job," Tab said jokingly, trying to ease his fears.

Her father looked up at her, and he knew she was right. "Honey, this could go so wrong," he told Tab, he looked over at his wife, and shook his head as he reached for the phone.

CHAPTER 8

Chandler

At the Pentagon, Roy's friend's phone began ringing. CIA Director and Head of Operations Chandler Barnett reached for the phone. "Hello," he said.

"Chandler, it's Roy Dawes. How have you been old buddy?" Roy asked.

"Great, Roy. So good to hear from you. I've just been very busy with this outbreak in Angola. It has us all running crazy. That is some really bad stuff over there. It's got everybody scared to death. No one knows anything about it," Chandler told his old friend.

"That's kind of why I'm calling. I've got some intel for you, but it needs to be face-to-face," Roy said.

"Concerning what, Roy? I am kind of busy right now. I was getting ready to fly out first thing in the morning. Can it wait a few days until I get back?" Chandler asked Roy.

"No, you need this intel right now. It concerns the outbreak. Send something to pick my daughter and me up," Roy told Chandler.

"Your daughter is coming with you?" Chandler asked.

"Yes, I will explain everything to you when we get there. Just hurry, I'm sure you know where to find me," Roy told Chandler as he hung up his phone. This last statement by Roy made Chandler smile as he leaned forward and hung up his phone.

Forty minutes later, Tab and her father were riding in a military helicopter high in the sky. Tab's father reached for her hand as she looked out the window.

"First time flying. I bet you're nervous, huh honey?" Her father asked her.

Tab looked at her dad and smiled. Right away, her father Roy realized this wasn't her first time flying. "Guess you've flown before. Did you pilot airplanes or helicopters?" her father asked, trying to be funny.

"Actually, Dad both, but I have always preferred flying helicopters over planes," Tab nonchalantly said as she turned to look at her astonished father. As Tab turned back toward the window, her dumbfounded father just smiled at her.

I guess that will teach me to try and be cute. I sure didn't see that one coming, he thought to himself.

"Who are we meeting with, Dad?" Tab turned to her father and asked.

"An old friend of mine," her father replied.

"Will he help us? I mean do you think he will believe us?" Tab asked.

"He's a good friend of mine, Tab. Let's just hope he hears us out before he throws us out. That'll be half the battle. Now buckle up. We're almost there," her father told her. The helicopter landed on the Pentagon grounds right next to several other even larger ones. Tab grabbed her fathers hand as they walked over to the building. Her father Roy walked in like he owned the place.

He knew the large building well as he led them down one corridor after another. Her father led her into an elevator where they went down seven levels. When the door to the elevator opened, her father led her down several more corridors. Then back into a second elevator where they went ten more levels below the ground. Wherever her father was leading her, it was deep within the structure. Tab joked that they should have brought their roller skates.

Finally, her dad stopped outside an office door. The sign on the door said, "Director of the CIA of the United States of America." Her father was hesitating, and Tab knew why. She knew he was worried about her safety.

Tab squeezed her father's hand, and in perfect Latin Tab told him, "Go on in, Dad. We'll be okay." Dad grabbed the door handle and held it for a second then turned it and went in. A very pretty young lady was sitting at a desk. Tab's father, went up to her and introduced them. Her name was Kacey, and she said it is very nice to meet them. They both returned her greeting. Tab's father told her that they were here to see her boss Chandler, and that he should be expecting them.

Kacey smiled and pushed a button on her desk phone. "Your guests are here to see you, sir," Kacey buzzed in and told Chandler. Chandler told her to please show his guest in. Chandler heard his door open and looked up to greet his guest.

"Roy, Tab, come on in and sit down," Chandler said as he got up to shake Roy's hand. He then turned his attention to Tab. "It's very nice to meet you Tab, and if you're wondering how I know your name, it's what I do," Chandler told her, trying to sound sly. Tab sensed he used that line a lot on new people he met. "So how was your flight? I hate flying in those helicopters. Your flight was good, I hope?" Chandler asked his guest.

"Yes," both Tab and her father answered as Chandler continued.

"So Roy, what have you got for me?" Chandler asked as he suddenly thought of Tab sitting next to her father.

"Oh, sorry Tab, would you prefer to sit outside in the lobby while your father and I talk? There is a television and—" Chandler said, but was cut short as Roy interrupted him.

"She is the reason we are here. She is the intel," Roy told him.

Chandler looked at Tab and then back at Roy. "How does your young daughter know anything about this outbreak? I haven't got times for games, Roy! I missed a flight to meet with you," Chandler said in a very annoyed tone. Tab was taken aback momentarily by Chandler's sudden change in demeanor. Her father had his work cut out for him, Tab thought, after she heard Chandler. She wondered how her father would handle this.

Roy sat and thought for a minute then slowly leaned toward Chandler, "Are you a religious man?" he asked him point-blank.

"What?" Chandler asked, surprised by the question. "Well, I guess I am as much as anybody else. Why do you ask?" Chandler asked, wondering where this line of questioning was leading. "What does my religious beliefs got to do with any of this? You need to start making sense Roy," Chandler said as his patience began to run out.

Tab's father began the process and told Chandler the short version of everything Tab had told him. Roy held nothing back, and he told Chandler everything. He just laid it all out there. Tab watched Chandler's face as her father told him one thing after another. Tab tried to decipher if Chandler believed her father or if he was about to have them both threw out. Several times during everything her father told Chandler, he looked over at her in almost disbelief. Tab felt a little uncomfortable each time Chandler looked over at her. But Tab knew deep down how crazy it all actually sounded, so she just sat there and smiled each time he looked at her.

Over an hour later, her father finished up and declared, "Well, there it is." Her father sat back in his chair, obviously worn out from the stress of it all. Chandler just sat there. They could see he was thinking, but there was no expression on his face at all that gave them a clue as to just what he was thinking about.

Chandler reached for his desk phone and pushed a button on it. "Yes," Kacey answered.

"Kacey get Amara on the phone. Have her send Jeff and Kevin over to see me. Tell her I need them in my office right now," Chandler sternly told Kacey.

"Yes sir," Kacey said. Tab and her father looked at each other. Neither was sure what Chandler's intentions were by making that phone call.

Chandler looked over at Tab and then at Roy. "I am just not sure what to think about what you have told me, Roy. We have known each other for a very long time. I consider you a friend. It's the only thing keeping me from calling security right now and having you both arrested for wasting my time!

"Still, it was a very interesting story, unbelievable but interesting just the same. So instead of having security remove you two, I am going to test your story. See if it holds water. Besides, it seems like such an easy story to disprove," Chandler said as he looked right at Tab.

"So you claim to know every language ever spoken since the beginning of time? Well, little girl, we will see. This is the United States Pentagon. We have people here who really can speak almost every language on the planet," Chandler said all this with an almost-arrogant prove-you-wrong tone.

Tab's father reached for her hand and held it as they waited. Tab looked up and gave him a nervous smile. He silently said a little prayer to himself; he asked God to please help his little girl make it through whatever Chandler had in store for her and to, above all, please keep her safe. They did not have to wait long.

Kacey buzzed in that Chandler's other guest had arrived. Chandler asked Kacey to send them right in. The door opened, and in walked two very nice-looking middle-aged men. Chandler introduced Jeff and Kevin, who just happened to be brothers, to Tab and Roy.

Then he explained to the two men that Tab, the eighteen-year-old daughter of his good friend Roy here, claimed to know every language ever spoken since the beginning of time. Both men smiled when Chandler made that statement. Chandler then asked the two men to verify or disprove her extraordinary claim.

CHAPTER 9

The Test

Without hesitation, Jeff jumped right in and told Tab he was going to say something in a foreign dialect and that all she had to do was to tell him the country it was spoken in and in what language he had said it in. He told her she could even answer in English if she wanted to. He asked her if she was ready. He said it in such a way that everyone just knew he thought there was no way Tab would pass this test. Jeff started out in a language he was sure Tab could not know.

After he asked his question, Tab looked Jeff right in the eyes. "The country is Russia, and you're speaking in the language of Mansi," Tab told him. Only Tab did not say it in English; Tab said it back in the language of Mansi. Everyone could tell by the look on Jeff's face that Tab must have answered correctly.

Jeff continued, and next he tried was Sango from the Central African Republic. Tab nailed it. Igbo from Nigeria and once again Tab nailed it. Jeff then went through Swazi, Frisian, Kikongo, and several others. Each time, Tab answered Jeff correctly and in perfectly correct dialect, accent, and all. Jeff said he was done.

Next, it was Kevin's turn. Kevin went through several different languages as he tried his best to stump her with exactly the same results as Jeff. After Kevin gave up, Jeff motioned for Kevin and Chandler to follow him out of Chandler's office and into the hallway. Tab could tell Jeff was up to something.

As soon as the door closed, Tab's father looked over at Tab and smiled. "Good job, baby girl. You were awesome. That'll get their attention," her father whispered. The three men were gone for only a few minutes when Chandler came back in alone.

"Do you believe us now?" Tab's father asked Chandler.

"I have one more man that Tab will need to speak to," Chandler smugly answered Roy.

"Who now? Hasn't she proven herself?" Tab's father said, obviously irritated by Chandler's tone.

"She was very impressive—no doubt—but this next man should prove a little more difficult," Chandler replied.

The way Chandler said that last statement, Tab knew he was determined to have her proven wrong. They only had to wait a few more minutes until Kacey buzzed in that a Mr. Derek Hall had arrived to see Chandler. The door once again opened up, and in walked a little old man; by little, I mean he was a little person.

In he walked and right over to Tab and her father where Chandler introduced everyone. Chandler asked him if Jeff had spoken to him, and Derek responded that he had. With this, Derek turned to Tab, and the moment he spoke his first word to her, Tab knew why Chandler had seemed so confident and so sure she would fail. Derek tried to talk to Tab in a now-extinct language called Seroa.

It came from South Africa. It had not been spoken on earth for several hundreds of years. Derek asked Tab if she was married or single. Tab replied in Seora that she was single and that she was only eighteen. Tab then told him that he had not pronounced a couple of the words he had said to her correctly, and she explained to him how to do so properly.

Tab asked him if he knew any other extinct languages, but before Tab had even let him answer, she started speaking in other extinct dialects. Then after each one, she explained in English what she had been speaking and where it came from and even the time period it was spoken. Derek could only confirm a few of all the ones Tab had spoken. He confessed that he did not know any of the others. Derek told Chandler to hire her on the spot.

Chandler, with a beaten look on his face, told Derek he could go. Derek thanked Tab and told her how remarkable he thought she was. He even asked Tab to leave him her email, that he had so many questions that he would love to ask her. Needless to say, he seemed very pleased to have met her.

"Chandler, now you have to believe us. How else could she speak in so many dialects? Everything we are telling you is true," Tab's father stood up and said.

"Yes, Roy, but you're asking me to believe that God is personally trying to help Tab. That's a hard pill to swallow," Chandler replied back.

Tab looked deep into Chandler's eyes. "You said you believed in God. Then why is it so hard for you to believe that he would help us?" Tab asked Chandler.

"I don't have an answer to that question," Chandler simply and honestly said. He turned to her father Roy, and asked him if by chance, he had brought a copy of the manuscripts and his notes that he had talked about having made.

"Of course I brought them," Roy said.

"Good, let me have them. I want to look them over tonight. If that's okay?" Chandler asked. Chandler reached once again for the button on his desk phone. "Kacey, please call and get Roy and his daughter a room for the next couple of nights. Roy's a good friend of mine, so make sure it has all the bell and whistles. Oh yeah, and please secure them a ride to get there," Chandler told Kacey.

"Yes Sir Chandler, will that be all?" "Kacey asked.

"That will be all, Kacey. Thank you," Chandler replied. Chandler then told Roy to have Tab and himself both back here in his office around nine o'clock the next morning. He then grabbed Tab's hand and shook it softly. "So nice to meet you, my dear. You are a very impressive young lady," Chandler told Tab. Turning back to her father, he said, "You two go get some rest. We've all got a big day ahead of us tomorrow, I am afraid. And Roy, you two plan on hanging around for at least a couple of days? I want you two close in case I need you," Chandler told Roy.

"No problem. We can do that," Roy replied. Chandler walked them both to his door, and everyone said good night. Chandler told Roy that their ride would be waiting out front where they came in at. Tab and Roy both thanked him, and they started the long walk back out.

Tab and her father held hands as they retraced their steps back out of the depths of the Pentagon. "Well, we're not in straight jackets or in jail. I'd have to say that went as well as we could have hoped for," Tab's father, said.

"You were great Dad," Tab said.

"Me? No! You were the one that was great. Everything you did in there was amazing. The things you know and the things you say you've seen, Tab, it's all mind-blowing stuff. You're sort of living proof of reincarnation," Tab's father said.

The moment her father said the word *reincarnation*, Tab breathed a sigh of relief. *Reincarnation, it's the perfect explanation for how I know what I know. It's not the whole truth, but it isn't completely a lie either. And the best part is it keeps my heavenly alter ego out of the picture*, Tab thought to herself.

Tab looked up at her father and saw the stress on his face. "You look as tired as I feel. Let's just quit thinking about all of this tonight. As soon as we get to the motel room, I say we order us a pizza and just relax. We probably should eat before we call Mom because she loves us and wouldn't want us to starve to death. Then we can call Mom so she can quit freaking out, which we both know she is. Then we hit the hay," Tab told her father, seeing if he caught the call-Mom-after-eating joke.

"Sounds perfect, baby girl. You can count me in on that plan," her father replied. He smiled at her as he told her that because he knew Tab would be on the phone to her mother as soon as they got inside the room. Tab sure loved her mother.

Meanwhile back at Chandler's office, Chandler sat back down at his desk and called Kacey again. He asked her to come to his office. Kacey came in right away. Chandler motioned for her to take a seat. She sat down right across from his desk.

Chandler looked up at her over his glasses. "Is everything set?" he asked Kacey.

"Yes sir, and with all the bells and whistles. You will have eyes and ears on their room in about ten more minutes. The room keys will even have tracking devices in them," Kacey answered proudly.

"Tomorrow when they come here, I want everything they leave in their room to be bugged, *everything*," Chandler emphasized.

"Yes sir. We won't lose them," Kacey tried to reassure Chandler.

"I don't care about them. I care about her. I could search a thousand years and never find another one like her. I want our best team on these two. Get Brock and Matt and get them up to speed on the situation. Make sure they have all the info and the tracking codes on Roy and Tab. You know what to do," Chandler said, trying not to leave anything out.

"Already ahead of you on that, sir. Brock and Matt will be here at 0500," Kacey proudly told him.

"Woman, you are good," Chandler replied.

"I try sir. Anything else?" Kacey asked Chandler.

"That will be all Kacey," said Chandler without even looking her way.

"Thank you sir," Kacey said as she stood up and walked out of his office.

Chandler picked up the notes and manuscript Roy had left him. He wasn't reading them; he just held them up and was looking at them. *No way would I normally believe any of these fairy tales, but if Jeff, Kevin, and Derek, arguably, the three best linguist on the planet, if they couldn't disprove her claim of knowing every language on the planet, then even as unbelievable as it sounded, maybe she did,* Chandler thought to himself.

Hey, wait a minute. If she can speak every language, it would stand to reason she could possibly read or write any written text. That could come in very handy. I've got more thousand-year-old text and tablets than I have thousand-year-old people to talk to. And Atlantis, just its location or any proof it actually existed at all could be worth millions. This thought made Chandler smile like a kid in a candy store.

He paused. *The outbreak. Now there's one that could land me in the White House. If heat is the cure, then I will be a national hero when I tell the world how to beat it. Yes, sir, indeed. She is my golden ticket.*

47

Tab, my dear, you don't know it yet, but we have a long, long relationship ahead of us. Chandler smiled as he continued thinking of all the ways Tab could bring him power and money. The possibilities seemed endless.

Chandler looked down at his watch, and after seeing the time, he reached for his computer keyboard. He feverishly began typing on it. Suddenly on the screen in front of him, an empty motel room came into view. Just then, the door on the screen opened up, and in walked Tab and her father Roy, carrying a pizza. "Got you," Chandler said softly, almost in a whisper.

Tab and her father Roy, spent over an hour on the phone with Tab's mother Christina, after they got into the motel room. Christina had been so worried about how everything would work out. She felt so much better after she heard how the meeting had went. She told them she loved them and told them both to get a good night's sleep. They told her the same and that they were both going straight to bed as soon as they ate. As soon as they hung up, they made quick work of the pizza. Both Tab and her father sleepily crawled into their beds, and after a couple quick little prayers, both fell fast asleep.

Tab woke up before her father. Before getting out of her bed, she silently said good morning to her Heavenly Father God. Tab had a very nice little one-sided conversation with him and ended it with her usual "Thy will be done on earth as it is in heaven."

Tab saw there was a coffee machine on the dresser by the television. She quietly rose and started making a pot of coffee for her father. Tab turned on the television and found the local news channel WLEX Fourteen and watched the morning news program. The news anchorman Dan Allen was once again talking about the outbreak. This time, he said the United States Government claimed to have found a possible cure for the outbreak happening in Angola—that a press conference held at the White House minutes before had said just that. He also said that WLEX would replay the press conference in its entirety in just a few minutes. Tab rushed over to her father's bed to wake him up.

CHAPTER 10

The Press Conference

"Dad, wake up Dad," she said, pushing on her father.

"What, what baby girl?" he sleepily replied.

"Wake up Dad, you have to see this. The news is saying the White House has found a cure for the outbreak. They're getting ready to replay the press conference," Tab said as she sat down by her father.

Her father, still half asleep, sat up. "How in the world? What did they say the cure was?" her father asked, still rubbing the sleep from his eyes. Tab made them both a cup of coffee while they waited for the press conference to replay. As soon as Tab and Roy took the first sips of their coffee, the replay of the press conference came on.

Both Tab and her father nearly spit out their coffee when they saw who was standing at the podium and getting ready to speak. It was Chandler, and he was standing in front of the UN Council getting ready to speak to a worldwide audience on television. And when he started speaking, he told the world, word for word, about how heat would destroy the blue boil affliction. He confidently spoke as if it was a proven fact and not just what it was—a simple theory.

When Chandler finished speaking, as expected, the first question he was asked was how he knew all of this. Chandler, being who he was, had the perfect reply to that question. Chandler spoke in his most professional voice and said, "As head of the CIA, I am not at liberty to disclose that information. I will say this though: America and the world still have a lot more to do to eradicate this horrifically contagious and killer disease. Maybe the worst disease the world has ever seen. Thank you, but I have nothing further to say at this time. Thank you," Chandler said as questions started flying his direction. He graciously excused himself and quickly walked away from the podium.

Both Tab's and her father's jaws were still on the ground as they turned and just stared at each other. Each one amazed at how fast Chandler had ran with their intel.

Tab finally broke the silence. "I'd say he believed us," Tab declared.

"Yeah, I may need to open up a car lot and sell used cars on the side. I never thought we would sell your story to Chandler. I was just happy when we didn't go to jail," Tab's father told her. Tab and her father hugged excitedly. "That was so much easier than I thought it was going to be. We make a great team, Tab," her father said.

"Yes we do, Dad. That was pretty easy," Tab said as she smiled ear to ear. All of a sudden as she pulled away from hugging her father, something dawned on her and a sense of clarity surrounded her. Just as Tab knew her earthly father Roy, would love some coffee this morning, she also knew something of this magnitude that concerned her Heavenly Father God would certainly not be so easily accomplished. *No way is this over. There has to be more,* Tab thought.

After Tab and her father got dressed, they grabbed the motel's grand continental breakfast. A doughnut and another cup of black coffee. Soon, they were walking back down into the depths of the United States Pentagon building again. This time, her father did not hesitate at Chandler's door but walked right in. Kacey smiled and pleasantly greeted both Tab and her father, Roy. She then got on her speaker phone and told Chandler that his guest had arrived.

"Please send them in," Chandler asked her.

As if Tab and her father Roy hadn't heard Chandler on the intercom, Kacey turned, "He said to please go on in," Kacey said with a big friendly smile.

"Thank you," Tab and her father both said in unison as Tab's father led the way into Chandler's office.

"Did you two see my press conference this morning with the UN?" Chandler proudly asked even before they sat down.

"Yes we did, and frankly speaking, it surprised us both with how fast you ran with our theory. Don't you think you should have tested the theory first before you told the world you had a cure?" Roy questioned Chandler.

Chandler came back fast at Roy. "The world needed an answer, and right or wrong, I gave it one. Right now as we are speaking, I'm sure the world's best minds are coming up with a plan to somehow try out the heat theory. Making the plan work is not my department. The beauty of this department is if we are ever wrong, then all I have to say is 'I guess we were given some bad intel.' And it never ever goes any further," said Chandler with a smirky look on his face.

Suddenly, Kacey buzzed in on the speaker phone, "Sir, you have an emergency call on line 7 you need to take now," Kacey intensely told him.

"Thank you Kacey," Chandler said as he picked the phone up from his desk. "Hello, Chandler speaking." Suddenly, his tone changed. "When did this happen! Has there been any word, any communication at all? You tell them I will personally handle this. If he is still alive, I will bring him back," Chandler said as he hung up the phone.

Tab couldn't help herself. "Is who still alive?" she asked Chandler.

Chandler, whose mind had already begun racing a hundred miles an hour, answered without thinking.

CHAPTER 11

President Down

"The president. The president's transport Air Force One went down somewhere over the middle of the Congo Basin. This is bad. The area he went down in is very remote, very dangerous, and hard to get to. Approximately 1.3 million square miles of mostly uncharted, unchanged rainforest filled with every kind of predator animal, venomous snake, or poisonous plant life known to man," Chandler accidentally told Roy and Tab.

"What's the local population like, friendly or hostile?" Roy asked Chandler.

"They still have headhunters in that area. It will be like going back in time to try and rescue the president. Everything is almost just as it was a thousand years ago. That is if he is even still alive to rescue," Chandler said, still in shock.

"I'm sorry, but you two will have to excuse me. I have a lot to do, and I am not even sure what that is yet. I just don't get it. The president's plane is the most sophisticated airplane ever built. Not even a rocket is supposed to be able to bring it down. It would almost take an act of God to bring it down. I need to be alone to think," Chandler said, his mind already deep in thought.

"Of course, we'll stay in town at the room you got us until you get this fixed. You do what you need to do," Roy told Chandler.

Tab and her father stood up to leave when something suddenly came over Tab, and she turned back, facing Chandler. "I know this much. If you're going to save him, you're going to need my help. I know that area better than anyone, and I can speak all the different languages they speak in that area, and they speak dozens in that region," Tab confidently told Chandler.

"Tab, no way you're going," her father told her.

"I have to Dad. It's the only way, and you know it," she pleaded back to her father.

"You know this area better than anyone?" Chandler asked her. "Please tell me how you know so much about apparently everything? You're eighteen for goodness's sake," Chandler exclaimed loudly.

"I just do, and I think your best chance of rescuing the president is to take me with you," Tab confidently told Chandler.

Roy looked at Chandler, "She is not going. She is too young, and she is not trained for the field," Roy told Chandler sternly.

"Roy, I am sorry, but it's the president of the United States of America we are talking about here, and if she thinks she can help, I am afraid I must insist she go along," Chandler apologetically said.

Roy was extremely frustrated, but he knew he was not going win this fight. "Okay, then if she goes, I go," Roy told Chandler. Roy looked at his daughter and shook his head. "What have you gotten us into, baby girl?" her father asked her.

"Sorry Dad, but I was compelled to offer my help. It just seemed like the right thing to do," Tab apologetically told him.

"Good, it's settled then. Roy, you and Tab head down to the DO. You know what to do. I need you two ready in case we have to go. I have got to scramble something close by and try to get eyes and ears on the scene. Maybe they can locate him or at least pinpoint where the president's plane went down," Chandler told Roy and Tab as his mind started firing on all cylinders. "Roy, thank you and Tab, thank you so much for offering your support. Hopefully, we'll find him, and none of us will even have to go," Chandler told Roy and Tab. Roy nodded his head and turned to walk out. "Good to have you back, Roy," Chandler said.

Roy immediately turned back toward Chandler. "Not back old buddy, just helping you out this one time, and that is all! Then both my daughter and I are done." Roy paused, still staring eye to eye with Chandler. "Both of us are going home," Roy sternly said.

Chandler understood Roy's concern and played dumb. "Well, of course Roy," Chandler replied.

Roy, still staring a hole through Chandler, mouthed again, "Both."

Chandler, to show he fully understood, told Roy, "Okay, I get it, both. You two help me get the president back, and you'll have my word I will leave you two alone." Roy gave Chandler one more stern look before he and his daughter Tab, walked out of Chandler's office. They told Kacey good-bye on their way past her as they entered the corridor on their way to the DO.

"Where are we going, and what exactly is the DO, Dad?" Tab asked her father. Tab's father smiled and took her hand as they hurried on their way.

"The DO is way on the opposite side of the Pentagon from where we are at now. The DO is where all of the agents go to 'Dress Out' for their missions. It's where they put on all their gear and pick out weapons or special equipment that they may need," her father, told her.

"What are we going to take with us? What will we need in the Congo?" Tab asked her father Roy.

"You're going to dress out in black jungle gear with a bulletproof vest and wear several tracking devices in case I lose you. Me, I'm taking everything I can carry because I can't let anything happen to you, or your Mom will kill me," her father, said, laughing as he tried to lighten the mood.

"You take what you want to Dad, but all I need is my faith, and I have enough faith for both of us Dad," Tab confidently said.

"I bet you do baby girl, but I'm going to bet that your mother would want me to take a weapon with me. Maybe several, that is if she knew where I was taking you," her father Roy said.

Tab agreed, "Yeah, this might be something Mom doesn't ever need to find out about," Tab suggested.

In the meantime, Chandler had been relentless on the phone as he made several calls in a matter of minutes. He ordered low-level flyovers in the sector of the jungle that the president's plane went down in. He notified the Congo government of the situation and of the emergency rescue attempt happening on their soil. He even had an elite special forces team heading toward the crash scene. Chandler even called Kacey and had her cancel Brock and Matt's surveillance duties. Chandler had done all this in the fifteen minutes it had taken Tab and her father Roy to walk to the other side of the Pentagon.

One very long walk later, Tab and her father finally arrived at the DO department. Roy opened the door to the lobby and a very young-looking woman stood up from her desk.

"Long walk from over there, isn't it?" the young lady commented. "It sure was," Tab replied.

The young lady introduced herself as Candy, and Tab and her father Roy in return, introduced themselves. Candy explained that Chandler had phoned ahead with instructions to allow them free reign to gear up and take anything they thought they may need for their assignment—also that she was to make sure before they left the DO that she gave them each all the shots they would need to safely go to the Congo jungle.

"Thanks, I think," Roy said, thinking about the shots. "Can you help my daughter Tab here, and get her outfitted with black jungle gear and with a bulletproof vest. Give her a couple of knives and a machete. Also a radio headset and some night vision goggles and put several tracking devices in her equipment and on her. Oh yeah, please get her a watch, and no matter what, positively no guns or anything explosive," Roy told Candy.

"Yes sir," Candy answered Roy. She then turned to Tab. "Follow me Tab, and I'll get you fixed up," Candy told Tab with a big smile on her face. Candy reached for Tab's hand, and they walked into the women's locker room. Roy watched the door close behind the girls. He wondered what Tab had got them into. He checked his watch then headed into the men's locker room.

Both Tab and her father had almost finished gearing up when Chandler's voice came over the intercom, "Roy, you and Tab pick the pace up. Looks like we will have to go after all. Start making your way to hangar 7 to the newly modified helijet. We roll in fifteen minutes." Chandler's voice blared out from the over head speakers.

Roy looked up at the ceiling, and in a really loud voice, told Chandler, "We'll be there!"

At the same time Roy came out of the men's locker room, Tab and Candy came out of the women's locker room. Candy told Roy she had already given Tab her vaccinations and that now it was his turn. Roy started to roll up his sleeve when Candy stopped him and told him it wasn't his arm she would be needing. Tab turned her head as her father got his vaccination shots.

Candy told them both how nice it was to have met them as Roy was redressing. Roy told Tab they had to hurry or they would miss their ride. Candy leaned into Tab and gave her a big hug and told her to be safe, and she promised she'd email her. Tab was still saying good-bye as her dad was leading her out the door by the hand.

They were almost running trying to make it on time, and luckily, the hangar was close by. Chandler was standing on the back of the cargo ramp of the helijet, looking at his watch. Tab and Roy did not even bother to stop as they ran past Chandler and went inside and hurriedly sat down and buckled up. Tab leaned over to her father and said how cool it was; she had never rode in a half helicopter and half jet plane before.

A few minutes later, they were airborne, and the only ones on board besides Roy, and Tab were the two pilots, Chandler, and three very big soldiers each armed heavily from head to toe. They all sat completely silent for about an hour. During this time, Tab's father gave Tab's mom a quick phone call.

Roy told her mother, Christina, they were going to travel to a really remote area to speak with some people and that they may not have phone service for a few days but not to worry; they were both in good hands, and he told her they would call her as soon as possible. After Roy hung up, once again everybody sat in silence, and although everyone looked each other up and down, no one said a single word.

Tab could clearly see all three of the really large soldiers' dog tags hanging around their very large necks, one said "Tracks," one said "Anvil," and the last one around, the biggest soldier's neck, just said "Bull." Finally, Chandler unbuckled and stood up, and he told everybody to do the same. First thing he did was introduce everybody to one another. Chandler introduced the biggest of the three soldiers first.

CHAPTER 12

The Guardians

"This is Brandon. We call him Bull. Bull is a corn-fed Hoosier from Anderson, Indiana. And as you can see, they grow them big in Indiana," Chandler said as Bull stuck out his very large hand to shake Tab's with. It was so big it was like putting her hand up against a catcher's mitt.

Tab noticed Bull had a small tattoo of a cross just below his thumb. Tab could tell it had been done by a really good artist. Although it was small, it was very detailed and very beautifully done. Tab wondered why he had gotten it.

Chandler said Bull was an expert in demolitions among many other things. Bull was a soft-spoken, enormous black man. But for such a big man, he had the softest voice ever when he told Tab and Roy, how nice it was to have met them. Tab sensed right away that Bull had a very big heart also.

Next, Chandler introduced Chris Thomas. "We call him Anvil. He's the best there is with knives or hand-to-hand combat," Chandler said. Anvil was of Mexican heritage and was from Hollywood, California. He was a very handsome man, with a big square-looking jaw.

This man could have easily been a male model as well as a soldier. Anvil had a very strong handshake, and he nearly accidentally broke Tab's hand when he shook it. Tab noticed that Anvil had the exact little cross tattoo that Bull had and in the exact same spot. She wondered if the third soldier would have it also.

As Anvil shook Tab's hand. they looked deep into each other's eyes. Right away. Tab could tell that Anvil was a highly courageous, very loyal type of man. Tab could feel goodness coming from inside his big beautiful brown eyes. She knew right then that as long as he had breath in his lungs that he would try his best to protect her and her father.

Lastly, Chandler introduced Andrew Skyler. "We call him Tracks. He's a good old country boy from Salyersville, Kentucky," Chandler boasted. Tracks had a very country ascent when he spoke, and Tab just loved his country draw when he told her it was nice to meet her. When Tracks shook Tab's hand, sure enough, right below his thumb was the exact same little cross tattoo.

Tab knew her curiosity would soon get the best of her, and she would have to know the story behind why they all three had the same little tattoo, and why a cross? Like the other two, when Tracks was shaking her hand, she had this almost overwhelming feeling of goodness, loyalty, and faith. She could sense Tracks's incredible faith deep within him the second his hand touched hers.

Chandler described Tracks as part Indian and part bloodhound; he said he could track a three-day-old trail in a thunderstorm. Tab knew one thing about them. No matter what they did as soldiers; they were all three good men inside where it counted. Tab silently thanked her Heavenly Father God for putting these three men in her path.

"Now that every body here has been properly introduced. let me tell you why you're all here with me at thirty thousand feet above the earth. It seems at ten thirty this morning. Air Force One went down somewhere in the Congo Basin with our president, President Richard Worsham on board, along with his entire security staff. The forest canopy is so thick in that region that even with coordinates from the black box on board, we only found the wreck site approximately forty minutes ago. Fifteen minutes ago, we finally got soldiers on the ground," Chandler told everyone.

Chandler held up a remote control and pushed a button, making a large monitor from the ceiling drop down. "This was what they found when they got down through the canopy and made it over to the president's plane," Chandler told them. The video was showing dead people outside and inside of the aircraft. "Every single body is accounted for except the president's," Chandler exclaimed as everyone stared in awe at the video.

"Here's an interesting sidenote to all of this: Several of the victims dead outside of the aircraft were part of the president's secret service staff. And they all were killed not from the wreck or by gunfire but apparently from arrows and blow darts," Chandler told the astonished group.

Surprised by that intel, everybody looked at each other with a blank expression. Chandler continued, "Make no mistake about the difficultness of this mission. We are dealing with over a million square miles of untouched, unchanged landscapes, animals, and tribal people apparently armed with arrows and blow darts. Thick jungles, mountainous terrain, and caves are going to make this rescue attempt next to impossible," Chandler told everyone.

"Do you think he is still alive?" Bull asked.

"Until we have his body, this is a rescue mission. Alive or dead, this mission isn't over until we bring him or his body out of that jungle. Is that clear, soldiers?" Chandler replied sharply.

"Yes sir," everybody said in unison, even Tab and Roy said it loud and clear.

"Everybody, get set to repel. We are less than ten minutes from our target zone. Bull, you take Tab down with you. Don't drop her like you did the last girl you took down. We need this one," Chandler said jokingly. Chandler looked at Tab, whose eyes were wide with doubt. "Just joking, Tab," he mouthed.

"He-haw," said Bull as he turned to Tab and smiled at her. "You're in safe hands with old Bull. You know I wouldn't drop you," Bull told Tab.

Tab reached over, putting her small hand on his huge paw. "I know you wouldn't drop me Bull. I trust you," Tab replied. Big Bull just sat there with a big smile on his face after he heard what Tab had said. Bull liked the attention his new little friend Tab had given him.

Suddenly, the overhead monitor lit back up, and Special Forces by the book, Asian-American Captain Steve Butler appeared. "Sir, my men have the hole cut in the canopy as requested. Base camp is up and operational. The perimeter is being set as we speak, sir," said the captain.

"Good job, Captain. We'll be dropping down momentarily," Chandler said.

"Sir yes sir," said the captain, saluting as the monitor went dark.

Standing by the open door of the helijet as it hovered above the hole in the treetops just made by the Special Forces team, they all could clearly see a beautiful, majestic, and ancient volcano mountain off in the distance.

Hello old friend, Tab thought to herself. Tab knew this volcano intimately. They each looked at its beauty as, one by one, they started repelling to the jungle floor. First Tracks, then Anvil, next Bull and Tab piggybacked down together. Tab prayed the whole way down. Then Roy went, and last to go was Chandler.

Once on the ground as he disconnected both himself and Tab from the drop cable, big old Bull looked down at Tab smiling.

"I told you I wouldn't drop you," Bull said proudly. Tab turned to face Bull and reached up, putting her small hand to Bull's face.

She smiled back at him. "I never doubted you for a minute," Tab told Bull. This made Bull feel like a king. Tab had always been amazed at how much joy the littlest acts of kindness could sometimes bring. Seeing Bull so happy momentarily made Tab forget they were on a rescue mission in hostile territory.

Chandler's voice brought her back in a snap as he hit the ground yelling out orders, telling everyone to meet inside the biggest of the three tents set up. Tab's father rushed over to her to make sure she was all right. He grabbed her by the hand, and they ran to the tent together. On the way, Tab silently thanked God for everyone making it safely to the ground.

Once inside the tent, Captain Butler gathered everybody around a large map of the area they were in. He explained to Chandler and to everybody that he had sent two separate two men teams out on recon missions as soon as they hit the ground trying to find the missing president. The trail of whoever had taken the president led north.

The captain pointed to the map to show the approximate direction the trail led away from the president's wreckage.

The captain continued as he told everyone that neither team had yet found the President nor has either team encountered any resistance in their search to find him. He also noted that with the heavy rain, the trail that led away from the wreckage had slowly gotten harder and harder to follow until neither team could find it at all. Chandler spoke up and told the captain to bring his teams in for the night. He told the captain about Tracks and how good he was at tracking.

"He'll find the trail. I promise you that," Chandler told him.

Tab joined the conversation, "Can I see the arrows and darts you found, please. Maybe I can tell you who took him and where they are taking him." Tab asked.

"You can do that just by looking at the arrows and the darts?" Chandler asked in disbelief.

"Oh yes, the markings on every tribe's arrows and darts tell everything about the people that made them. No two tribe's markings are ever the same," Tab told Chandler.

Captain Bulter told one of his soldiers to go fetch one of each for Tab to look at. Soon, Tab was examining the arrow and the dart, and right away, she knew the tribe who had made them.

CHAPTER 13

The Manduno

"This arrow and dart were made by the Manduno tribe. One of the largest and oldest tribes in the Congo Basin," Tab said loudly so everyone in the tent could hear her.

"The Manduno tribesmen are fierce warriors. Most of the other tribes are afraid of them in this area and try to stay clear of them. They are a tribe of headhunters. The Manduno are a very wise people, and it has been speculated they are so wise because they are known to eat the brains of their captured victims, thus somehow gaining their enemies knowledge and secrets through this brutal act," Tab told everyone as they attentively listened.

"I can also tell you that they are more likely than not here right now watching our every move. The warriors are masters of camouflage and blending into their environment. Lucky for us, I just happen to know where they call home. Their village has always been here," Tab said, pointing to the huge volcano on the map—the same beautiful volcanic mountain they had all just seen from the door of the helijet before they repelled to the jungle floor.

The volcano sat at the southern edge of a very large mountain range near the southern boarder of the Congo Basin on the big map. "If they have him, as I believe they do, then I know where they will most likely keep him. I also know of a secret way into that area through a cave system that no one but the Manduno people knows about, so it's never guarded," Tab told everybody.

"How do you know all of this?" the captain asked.

"I just do," said Tab.

Chandler interrupted, "She's here for everything she does know about this area and about the people who live here. She's a CIA secret, so let's all leave it at that. It's on a need-to-know basis, and none of you need to know," Chandler sternly told the captain and everybody in the tent!

"Sir, she's saying that the Manduno village is due south, but the trail leading away from the wreckage led north, sir," the captain stated, looking at Chandler.

Chandler replied back to the captain, "This little girl has yet to be wrong even once since I've met her, Captain, but at daybreak, I'll let you, Tracks, and four of your men follow the trail north. I'll take my crew and your other four men south with me straight to the Manduno village.

"If Tab is wrong, then Tracks will lead you and your men to the president. If Tab's right, then Tracks will follow the trail north until it doubles back to the south, which should lead you all back down to us," Chandler said pointing at the huge volcano on the map.

"Either way this goes down, if your team or mine gets eyes on the president and he is not in mortal danger, then we wait until we can rally together and do this as a team. Is that clear?" Chandler asked everyone in a really loud voice.

"Clear," everyone shouted back!

The captain pulled Chandler to the side, "Sir, permission to speak freely, sir," the captain asked.

"Of course Captain. Go ahead," Chandler answered.

"Sir, are we being led by a little girl? What makes you think she's right, sir?" the captain asked, sounding a little agitated by the thought.

"Two things Captain: first, Tab is an expert on this area and these people, and second, you said your men met no resistance on a hot trail. Who doesn't guard their flank when they know they will surely be followed, Captain? It had to be a ploy to lead us in the wrong direction, and my guess is they probably are heading south. If Tab's right about them being such fierce warriors, then we better be ready for a fight when we catch up to them," Chandler told the captain.

"Sir, they use bow and arrows and blow darts. My men carry M16 machine guns," the captain started telling Chandler when Chandler interrupted him.

"Captain, they killed five of the president's highly trained secret service agents with those darts and arrows. And even though we are all wearing bulletproof vest, I will bet you that every single blow dart and arrow they have is dipped and laced with some kind of tree frog poison or who knows what—one stick and you're probably dead. They, the enemy, know this forsaken terrain better than you know your hometown. And here's the big problem: we don't even know their numbers. There could be ten of them, or there could be ten thousand of them just waiting on us to come try and rescue the president. Make no mistake Captain. We are in for the fight of our lifetime. And that little girl you're questioning, she may just be our only hope of getting through all of this alive," Chandler told the captain.

The captain said the only thing he could to Chandler after hearing everything he had to say, "Sir, yes sir."

Chandler stepped back into the circle of soldiers who were still looking at the huge map. He held his arm up to show everyone his watch.

"It won't be daylight until 0700 hours, so be locked and loaded and ready to go by then, and everyone bring you're 'A' game. This isn't going to be easy," Chandler emphasized to everyone. The captain called all his men outside. He knew they had a lot of work to do before it got totally dark. They needed to finish setting up the perimeter security.

Once the Captain and his men walked outside, Chandler started going over the game plan for tomorrow with his team. He told Tracks to follow the trail leading north. To see if it was a ploy to lead them wrong or if it was for real. Either way, he said he wanted Tracks to follow it until it ended or took him to the president.

If the trail turned south and headed back toward the volcano Tab had showed them on the map as he said he thought it would, he wanted their team to rendezvous with his team at the river just north of the volcano. Chandler pointed at the map to show Tracks exactly where he wanted them to meet him. He explained to Tracks and everyone that they had three good radios, two CB fifteen-mile radios and one long-range satellite radio. Tracks and the captain was to take a CB fifteen-mile radio with their team and stay in constant communication with him. The other CB fifteen-mile radio and the long-range satellite radio would remain with him and his team.

He then turned to Bull and Anvil and told them to let the Special Forces team take the lead tomorrow. He explained to them that their job was to protect their flank as they traveled through the jungle to the volcano mountain that the Manduno tribe called their home. Chandler told them he did not want any surprises sneaking up on them.

Next, he turned to Roy and Tab. "Roy, your job is to just keep your daughter Tab, safe. She was right. I'm afraid we are certainly going to need her," Chandler told Roy. Then, looking at Tab, Chandler told her, "Under no circumstance are you to be left alone on this mission or go wondering off. Last thing we all need would be to have to rescue you and the president. Is that clear, Tab?"

"Very clear, sir," Tab reassured him.

"Why would they take a hostage? Why the president and no one else?" Chandler changed the subject and asked Tab.

"They probably watched the president giving orders after the crash or seen how his staff treated him like royalty. They most likely were hidden in the undergrowth close enough to touch the president when they grabbed him. I'm sure the agents they killed never even seen them. To capture a king or royalty to the Manduno is a great honor.

"They will keep the president alive and treat him very well for about one week. Then they will behead him, eat his brains, and shrink his head to the size of a softball. It will be a cherished trophy to the Manduno people," Tab told Chandler and everyone. Every one looked at each other and just shook their heads at what Tab had just told them.

Chandler looked over at Roy, and Roy could almost hear him ask "How does she know all of this?" with the way Chandler looked at him. Roy just shook his head and shrugged his shoulders in response to Chandler's look.

"Alrighty then. We have a week, we have a plan, and we have her," Chandler said as he looked over at Tab. "Everybody not on watch, try and get some sleep," Chandler told everybody. He then turned to Tracks and Anvil. "You two take the first watch. Bull, you and Roy take the second watch. Two-hour intervals and no one is to go anywhere alone. No one but me is to leave this tent," Chandler sternly told everyone. Everyone nodded okay.

Chandler walked outside. He stopped and cautiously looked around. It was only about 1700 hours, but it was already nearly to dark to see outside. Even though it was only late afternoon, the jungle canopy almost completely blocked out the sky, allowing almost no sunlight to come through and reach the ground. The captain and his men had almost finished setting up the perimeter security: three hundred sixty degrees of motion sensors, all with heat-sensing capability to protect the camp. Chandler walked over to the captain and reminded him what Tab had said about them probably being watched and told him to stay alert.

"No lights of any kind are to be used outside, Captain. You and your men are to use night vision equipment only," Chandler quietly told the captain.

The captain immediately told his men through his headset radio, "Lights out, ladies. Cat eyes only, and make them red." This was how the captain told his men to use their night vision goggles and to also use their heat-sensing capabilities.

The captain told Chandler to follow him back inside the main tent. Once inside, the captain walked over to a small monitor and keyboard on the only table in the tent. He started typing on the keyboard, and suddenly a very dimly lit screen came on. To their surprise, several red figures were seen moving very slowly and deliberate about twenty yards out beyond their perimeter security. Even though they were in complete darkness, the motion sensors and heat sensors the soldiers had installed tracked each one of them as they slowly split up and began to encircle the camp.

The captain used his two-way headset radio to notify his men outside. "We got company—twenty yards out in every direction and closing. There are eight total, and you have the green light to take them out," the captain almost whispered and told his men. Tab heard what the captain had told his men, and she knew she had to do something.

"No, please let me try and make them go away. I have an idea I think will work. Please let me try," Tab pleaded.

The captain looked over at Chandler. "Let's see what she's got," Chandler whispered.

"Stand down unless you are attacked," the captain told his men via his headset radio.

"Have you got a loudspeaker or something I can speak to them with?" Tab asked the captain.

The captain hit a button on his keyboard and handed Tab a small microphone. "Here. Will this do?" he said.

"Perfect. Will you please turn it up really loud?" Tab asked him. The captain did as he was asked and turned it up as loud as it would go. He then looked back at Tab and nodded it was ready.

Tab grabbed the microphone and held it close to her mouth and started speaking the language of the Manduno people. Both the captain and Chandler intensively watched the monitor. The second Tab started speaking, every red figure on the screen stopped moving. As Tab started getting into whatever it was she was telling them, she started moving her hands and arms wildly, even making faces.

Suddenly and at the very same time, every red figure on the screen started moving away very quickly until not a single one was left on the screen. Tab sat the microphone down and smiled.

"What did you say to them Tab?" her father asked.

"Whatever it was, they all left, and in a big hurry too," the captain said.

"I don't think they will be back tonight," Tab said still smiling. Tab answered her father, "The Manduno is a very superstitious people. They have many scary legends and prophecies that they pass down from generation to generation. One prophecy in particular terrifies every single one of the Manduno people," Tab said.

"What's that prophecy about, Tab?" Bull asked Tab.

"It's one of their end-of-times prophecies. They have a few end-of-times prophecies. This one is about a creature that they call Magra, which means 'the slayer that comes from the stars.' Once down in the jungle, it ferociously searches for the Manduno village. Along the way, it kills, beheads, and eats the brains of every man, woman, and child it comes upon.

"Once it finds the Manduno village, death and destruction follow for all of the Manduno people. The prophecy says none of them will survive the encounter with Magra," Tab told Bull and everyone. Tab paused and looked around the room at everybody. The entire room was hanging on to her every word.

She continued, "I simply played on their fears. I told them I was Magra, and I had come from the stars. I asked the warriors that were surrounding the white men to show me to their village, or I would behead them one by one and eat their brains while I destroyed their village," Tab told everyone. I told them I was so hungry from my long journey from the stars." Tab knew that last statement would get to the warriors.

Bull started laughing. "Good job Tab. You scared them half to death," he said smiling.

Tab felt bad about tricking the warriors outside, but she knew it was far better to scare them off than it was to allow them to be slaughtered. Tab knew scaring the warriors with the prophecy would work. Twice, she had lived a life as a Manduno woman. The last time for ninety one long years she lived with the Manduno people.

She had heard that prophecy so many times as a young girl, and it scared her every time she heard it. As she got older, she told the same prophecy herself more often then she had heard it as a child, first to her children then to her grandchildren and still yet to her great-grandchildren. She remembered how scared the story always made all her babies feel each and every time they heard it.

Tab smiled, thinking about how silly it all sounded to her now. She started missing all her kids and grandkids and that life she had lived back then as she was thinking about it all. And even though at times it was difficult, she really enjoyed her life with the Manduno people. They were such a hardworking, dedicated people.

The Manduno tribe is the largest tribe in the Congo Basin. Their size and reputation as fierce head-hunting warriors kept most other tribes away from them, so life with them for the most part was a peaceful, happy existence. No one in the tribe ever went without. The jungle is a bountiful place if you know what to eat and what not to eat.

There are untold medicines growing almost limitlessly all around you. The Manduno tribe has had many witch doctors, both men and women who have all been masters at telling what type of plants, roots, or fungi was needed for whatever might be ailing you. Normally, Manduno people died of accidents or predators, not of sickness.

If the world really knew all that the rainforest contained in them, they would stop cutting them down. God put everything in rainforest that humans need to thrive on this earth. The rainforest of the world hold so many wonderful, important, and amazing secrets yet to be revealed that it's a travesty how some humans just let greed get in the way and destroy so much of these beautiful untapped resources.

But then again, as always, it comes back to the drama. Tab smiled, thinking about this past life she lived out, and although it seemed like yesterday to her, it had been nearly three hundred years since she had been with the Manduno people. In total, she has lived forty lives throughout her trips to school here in the Congo Basin. She always loved the jungle environment and the freedom in the way the tribal people lived was and is so rare and so beautifully simple.

The captain brought her attention back sharply as he loudly said, "Story time's over boys and girls, and company is gone at least for now. Nothing has changed, and all orders stand. Go red or go to bed." With this said, the captain walked outside to be with his men.

Chandler sat back down in his chair in front of the monitor as soon as the captain went out the door. Chandler looked over at Tracks and Anvil, who were making a pot of coffee to help them stay awake. Chandler used the keyboard to pan the camera view in every direction as he looked for their recent unwanted guest; so far, they had not returned. He hoped Tab was right when she said she did not think they would be back tonight.

He wondered how she knew so much about so many things. He looked over at her sitting on the floor of the tent next to Roy and Bull. All three of them were nestled up against some bags of gear. Chandler knew there was something mighty special about Tab, and he hoped that they all stayed alive long enough for him to find out what it was.

Poor dad, Tab thought to herself as she watched him fade in and out of sleep. *No doubt he's been worried to death about me since we arrived. Dad is such a good man.* She hoped for her mother's sake that nothing happened to either of them. *They are still so much in love and they truly live for one another,* Tab thought, and even knowing the truth about everything, the thought of her mother being alone saddened her.

Bull, about half asleep himself, saw the sad look on Tab's face. He immediately reached out and lightly touched her shoulder. "You okay Tab?" he worriedly asked.

"I'm okay Bull. I was just thinking about things. For one, how is Dad sleeping with all this noise? It's louder now then when it was in the daytime. Normally, he has to have complete silence to even try to sleep," Tab replied as she looked up at Bull and talked about how loud the jungle was even during the nighttime.

"You can sleep through anything if you're tired enough, and your dad looked pretty tired. Anyway, you be sure to let old Bull know if you need anything," Bull caringly said.

"Thanks Bull, I will." She paused, remembering about the little crosses on all three of their hands. "There is one thing, Bull, something I'd like to know," Tab told him.

"What's that, little girl? What can old Bull tell you?" Bull said, smiling at her. Tab reached over and grabbed his big right hand and turned it over and pointed to the small cross located just below his thumb.

"What's this cross stand for, Bull? I noticed that all three of you have the same identical little cross tattoo. Does it mean something?" Tab softly asked Bull.

CHAPTER 14

The Tattoos

Bull hesitated in answering. Tab saw Bull's eyes tear up. Suddenly, she could actually feel Bull's pain. It was a heart-wrenching feeling he was having.

Bull looked down at Tab. "I never talk about it. I don't think the others do either, but I will tell you," Bull told Tab.

"You don't have to, Bull," Tab said. Bull took his left hand and rubbed the little cross as he looked down at Tab, with tears still in his big soft eyes. Bull began telling Tab the story of the little cross tattoos and how they come about.

"My squad and I were stationed in Kuwait. It was right before the second Gulf War. There were seven of us in the squad back then. We were all best friends. We had all seen and been through a lot together during the first Gulf War.

The seven of us survived dozens of secret missions behind enemy lines. We were more like brothers than friends really. From day 1, we all got along so well. Anyhow, it was just a typical day like so many others before it. My squad and I were out on patrol, just driving around doing more laughing than patrolling.

As always, we drove by this really old, huge orphanage. I looked forward to driving by it because all the little boys and girls would hear our big truck and always run to the windows to wave to us as we drove past them. The name of the orphanage was Home of God's Little Angels. We had even stopped several times and met all the children. Every time, the nuns would always give us bread and pastries when we stopped. We loved stopping as much as the kids loved it when we did.

On this particular day, just as we got to the turn off that heads to the orphanage, we heard the first explosion. As far away as we were, our windows rattled, and debris started raining down on our truck. As we speed up toward the orphanage, we could see the roof engulfed in flames. Thick black smoke filled the sky above it. Then a second smaller blast took all the windows out of the entire first floor.

"Right away, we all noticed not a single person, kid, or nun had run out of the orphanage. All seven of us ran right into the huge building not thinking about the fire and flames that were everywhere. Inside in the main living room, we found most of the kids and two of the nuns. The huge concussion from the first blast had apparently knocked them all out.

"The seven of us were each hauling two kids at a time outside, throwing them like sacks of potatoes up over our shoulders. The flames were starting to encircle us. We were literally running with them out of the orphanage and laying them all out on the ground under this twelve-foot-tall beautifully carved wooden cross that stood at the entrance to the orphanage. After a few trips, we had carried out every kid and nun we could find in the smoke-filled rooms of the orphanage.

"Tracks, Anvil, and I started performing CPR on two of the little ones that didn't appear to be breathing. The other four members of our squad ran back into the orphanage looking for anybody else that may have been left in the burning building. They had just disappeared inside the smoky doorway of the orphanage when the third massive explosion happened. It leveled the orphanage to the ground, instantly killing our four comrades," Bull said as a huge tear rolled down his cheek as he recalled the incident.

Tab reached over and took Bull's hand into her own. Tab was crying also; she was feeling every ounce of his pain as though they were somehow connected in all this. Bull continued, "The explosion was so great that it sent our large army convoy truck that was parked between us and the orphanage flying through the air right at us and all the kids that we had laid out on the ground. All three of us looked up just in time to see it coming.

"I remember praying to God thinking this was the end. But miraculously, that beautiful wooden cross, barely in the ground and leaning, stopped our big seven-ton metal truck from crushing all of us. God saved us and all those kids that day. So in honor of God and the miracle he bestowed on us all that day, the three of us went and each got these two matching tattoos," Bull told Tab.

"You three have two matching tattoos?" Tab asked looking up at Bull.

"Oh yeah, you haven't seen our other one," he said, wiping away still another large tear from his cheek. As he tried to pull his huge arm out of all the gear he had on, he explained that the designs on the little cross matched the carvings perfectly on the actual twelve-foot cross that saved their lives. "The very same one that still stands today out in front of the new orphanage that Tracks, Anvil and me helped build back so all the little kids would have a place to call home again," Bull said as he looked sadly at Tab.

"I love my little cross tattoo on my hand, but truthfully, my favorite is the one I'm trying to show you," big Bull told Tab. Finally, he got his arm out, and he turned and showed Tab the second tattoo. Tab was in disbelief. There on Bull's extremely large bicep was the most beautiful tattoo she had ever seen and what was wrote across the top of it blew her mind.

The tattoo was of a beautiful little girl, a toddler kneeling in prayer. The toddler had beautiful, large angel wings that had wrapped around her like a warm blanket. Standing above and behind her is the silhouette of three large soldiers all looking down at the little angel and each with their arms folded at their chest. The little angel is holding four sets of soldier dog tags in her hands as she is praying. A small teardrop is in the corner of the beautiful little girl's eye.

A tattoo banner with the encryption, "Guardians of God's Angels," is written above it all. "This one is in honor of the orphanage, the children, and our brothers that died that day," Bull said.

Bull leaned his big head down, and with a big teardrop still in his eyes, he very gently kissed the tattoo on his massive bicep. Tab looked one more time at the tattoo, and as Bull turned away to pull his gear back on, Tab quickly looked up and closed her eyes and silently started talking to God.

"Thank you, Father. You know my needs better than I do. Thank you for everything. I love and miss you so much. Oh yeah, thank you for sending my new soldier friends to help me. They are such good men, Father. Thank you so much for them and please protect us all on our mission. Please guide me as you see fit and as always, Father. Thy will be done on earth as it is in heaven." Tab opened her eyes as she finished talking to God.

Bull looked at Tab after he finished putting all his gear back on. "That's the first time I ever told anybody about any of that," Bull told Tab.

"Thank you for sharing that with me, Bull. Sometimes it helps so much just to talk to a friend and get things off of your chest," Tab told Bull.

"I do feel better. Thank you for listening. Now you better shut those eyes and try to get some rest," Bull softly told her.

"I will if you will." Tab replied.

Bull smiled and nodded. They both laid back against the bags of gear and closed their eyes to get some sleep. As Tab laid there trying to get some sleep, thoughts of being back in the jungle that she has called home so many times filled her mind. Tab loved the jungle. Tomorrow was going to be a great day.

CHAPTER 15

The Adventure Begins

Tab yawned and stretched, trying to wake up. She could see Chandler and her father, were up and drinking a cup of coffee sitting at the small table with the monitor on it. Tab turned to tell Bull good morning.

"He's already outside, Tab," her father told her, seeing her looking around for him. "Get up and get yourself awake. We'll be heading out soon," he continued.

"Good morning," Tab told them both as she stood up and made herself a cup of coffee. "Was there any trouble last night?" she asked.

"No, they never came back. You were right, baby girl," her father answered.

Finally, Chandler can't hold it in any longer. "How did you know so much about the Manduno tribe last night, all their personal information about their prophecies and their arrow markings? How in the world do you know so much about everything?" Chandler questioned Tab.

Tab looked deep into Chandler's eyes. "I already told you God was helping us. God is the answer to all of your questions whether you accept it or not. Everything I am trying to do and everything I know is by his hand," Tab assured Chandler, still holding eye contact with him.

"Girl, I make my living reading people and situations, and I'm very good at what I do. And as crazy as I may sound saying this, I am starting to believe there are powers at work here greater than us. Maybe God is at work here helping us. But when I read you, I know there's a whole lot more you're not telling us—a whole lot," Chandler knowingly told Tab.

"Everyone has their little secrets. I guess I am no different, but I'm here to help," Tab said.

"Fair enough. I can live with that answer for now. I guess I have to. For the record, I am a hard man to impress, and you've impressed me everyday since I've met you, young lady. You are something very special, and I really appreciate you and your father's help," Chandler told her. Chandler looked over at Roy to make sure that he had heard what he had told Tab. "I guess it's time to get this party started," Chandler said as he got up and headed toward the door.

As soon as Chandler, Roy, and Tab walked outside, Tracks and the captain walked over to tell them they were ready to head out. Chandler had everyone synchronize their watches before the two teams split up and headed out in different directions. Chandler also gave the captain one of the two fifteen-mile CB radios he had brought with him. Chandler told the captain to periodically check in with him and to let him know as soon as possible if they find the president.

Tracks, the captain, and four of his men then headed off north, following the original trail made by the Manduno warriors when they first took President Worsham. Chandler and the rest of his team headed south to the Manduno village at the base of the big volcano mountain—a good day-and-a-half walk from the base camp.

The temperature was a balmy 93 degrees with 90 percent humidity. The air was so thick with moisture it might have been easier to swim there than walk. A soldier named Otto, the captain's right-hand man, led the way. The captain's other three men stayed up front with Otto. Then there was Chandler, Tab, and her father Roy, followed by Anvil and Bull who brought up the rear.

All their headset radios were connected, so it gave Tab something to do, listening to all the cross talk between Chandler and the soldiers up front to the cross talk between Chandler, Anvil, and Bull in the rear. Several times, Bull came across asking Tab if she was okay. Tab would always smile and tell him she was fine. Tab liked the way Bull worried about her. Her father was the bad one because he never got more than three feet away from her.

He was so afraid something would grab her, bite her, or kill her that she finally had to turn and tell him, "Dad, I know you're worried about me, and I love you for that. Please don't ever stop worrying about me, but Dad, you're going to get hurt yourself if you don't start concentrating on what you're doing instead of what's about to get me. I'm okay. I'll be okay, and I know this jungle as well as I know my bedroom back home," Tab said as she threw her hand up. "It's a long story, Dad, a very long story," Tab told her father.

Tab leaned up and kissed her father on the cheek. And to prove her point, she grabbed a huge vine hanging from a tree and cut it into with one of her knives her father had Candy pack for her. Her father watched as she held the vine up to her mouth and took a big drink of jungle fresh water. She cut another one and held it up to her father's mouth. He placed his lips on it and drank several large gulps of fresh water.

"That's a new one on me," he said to Tab.

To further prove her point, she then pointed to a small but fat caterpillar climbing up a very large leaf. She picked it up between two of her fingers and held it up so her father could see it. She looked her father square in his eyes and placed the juicy little fat caterpillar in her mouth and started chewing. Moments later, she swallowed it, "Um, good, but kind of nutty," Tab said, smiling at her dad. She knew this would get him as she knew he had a very weak stomach.

Her father bent over and gagged and came real close to almost losing it. "Never do that again, or you're grounded," he said, still bent over. He looked up at Tab's big smiling face, and they both started laughing. Her father needed that laugh. Tab could sense his tension level coming down.

As they journeyed onward, Tab looked down at her watch It was close to ten in the morning. And as expected, here came the rain again. For the next hour, it poured down on them. It actually felt better with the rain; the temperature felt a good twenty degrees cooler with the rain. Almost better than the temperature feeling cooler was how the rain made all the mosquitoes disappear.

Suddenly, Tab's whole body began to tingle, and not being sure what was happening to her, she called out to her father.

He turned and ran back to her. "What's wrong, Tab? What is it?" her father asked her.

"I don't know, Dad. I'm tingling all over," Tab said as she leaned against her father, still not sure what was happening.

"Did something bite you, Tab?" her father worriedly asked.

"Oh, Dad, I know what it is. Now hang on to something. Quick," Tab said as she grabbed her radio headset microphone in her hands.

CHAPTER 16

An Old Friend Awakens

"Everyone, stop right now and take cover and hang on to something," Tab yelled into the microphone. Before anybody could even ask her what she was talking about it happened. The ground started shaking violently, and tree limbs and debris from the canopy started falling down all around them. A huge crack started opening up in the ground and ran right across their path. The ground shook so bad it threw Tab and her father off their feet. It stopped as suddenly as it had started. Chandler ran back to them and stopped at the new crack in the ground that now blocked his path.

"What was that, and how did you know that was going to happen?" Chandler excitedly asked Tab.

Tab looked over and answered him with both her and her father still flat on their butts. "I think that was the volcano we're all heading to. And to answer your second question, I got the strangest tingling sensation that came over me. And then I just knew that an earthquake was going to happen," Tab answered him. Her father, Roy, stood and reached down and helped Tab stand up.

"Wow, that was intense. Are you two okay?" Chandler yelled over the large rip in the ground.

"I think we're both okay. Maybe just a little shook up," Roy answered Chandler.

Chandler spoke into his radio headset, "Is everyone okay out there? Sound off?" he asked everyone. One by one, everyone radioed in and told Chandler they were okay. Chandler had Anvil and Bull come up to help Tab and Roy find a path around the huge crack in the ground that had now blocked their way. Chandler told Otto and the Captain's other three men to carry on.

Chandler then turned to Tab and Roy. "Good job, girl. Keep up the good work," he said.

"Credit goes upstairs on this one. It was all him," Tab said, giving her Heavenly Father God all the credit while pointing up.

Chandler looked up. "Thank you, Lord," he sincerely said as he turned back to Tab. "You're making a believer out of me, girl," Chandler told her as she just smiled back at him. Chandler then turned and headed on up the trail. The rain finally eased up some as Tab looked back and saw Anvil and Bull walking in their direction. Tab threw up her hand and waved to them. They saw her and her father and waved back.

Her father reached over and knocked off the dirt and debris from her back. "You really okay, baby girl?" he asked her.

"I'm good, Dad. Really, I'm fine," Tab said, trying to convince him. Anvil and Bull walked up and saw the huge crack in the ground.

"Wow, that's pretty cool. I never seen anything like that before," Bull said.

"Even cooler was how you knew that was going to happen. Thanks for the warning, Tab," Anvil told her.

"Yeah, thanks, Tab. You are an amazing young lady," Bull added.

"Thanks, you two, I appreciate everything you two have been doing for us, and I truly mean that," Tab told her two big soldier friends.

"We better hurry and find a way around this crack. It's safer if we all stay together as a group," her father told everybody. This time, Bull took the lead, and Anvil brought up the rear. The rip in the ground ran for a good two hundred yards before they found a place they could safely cross. They had just caught up with Chandler when the rain started coming down again. Anvil and Bull took their spot back at the rear. Tab and her father got back in line and stayed a good twenty yards behind Chandler. And once again, the small band of soaking wet rescuers was back on their way.

Meanwhile, ten minutes ago with the captain, Tracks, and their team, they were making really good time. They were all moving very effortlessly and quietly through the jungle. Tracks had a good eye on the trail The Manduno warriors had left behind. Luckily, Tracks had just motioned for everyone to hold up when it hit.

The earthquake had Tracks and everyone ducking for cover as the canopy rained down debris upon them. The ground seemed to buckle under their feet as tree after tree fell around the men, barely missing them. It only lasted a few minutes, and by the grace of God, except for a few scratches, no one was injured very badly. The captain immediately called Chandler on the CB radio and asked him if they had just felt the earthquake.

The captain then asked Chandler if everyone was all right. Chandler told him yes, that they had indeed just had an earthquake and that they were all okay. Chandler, in return, asked the Captain the same question, and he answered that everyone was fine. The captain said he would radio again as soon as he found anything out.

The captain put the CB back in his backpack and told everyone to take a few minutes to catch their breaths. The team, though shaken up a bit, only took a few moments to gather themselves and then got back on their way following the trail left by the Manduno warriors, a trail now hindered by debris and downed trees. Tracks had his work cut out for him now. He had a good line on the direction they had been traveling, and they had hardly veered from it. He was sure he could pick it back up somewhere up ahead.

Back to Chandler and Tab's team, Tab was working hard to stay on her father's heels. The pace the soldiers were setting up front was a very quick one, and Tab was finding it hard to keep up with them. The rain and all the heavy gear she was wearing had slowly started to wear her out. Tab hoped they would stop and take a break soon.

One good thing, the talk with her father must have worked because he hadn't stopped to wait on her or stopped to check up on her but a couple of times since then. Finally, the rain began to die down a little, and she could hear the captain's men on her headset radio. They were a good hundred yards ahead of everybody, and they told Chandler to catch up with them. They wanted to show him something.

The soldiers had stopped at a small clearing near the edge of a small overhang. From this viewpoint, you could look out over the canopy and see the vastness of the rainforest. The team could clearly see the huge volcano and the mountain range that connected to it even though it was still a good fifteen miles away. Only one big difference now jumped out at all of them about the volcano.

There was a thick, dark ash and smoke plume coming out of the top of the once-dormant volcano. One by one, all the others, Tab, her father Roy, Anvil, and lastly Bull came up to the group to admire the view.

"That can't be good," Chandler said, looking at the plume of smoke coming out of the volcano.

"The earthquake we felt earlier must have triggered the volcano," Otto, the captain's right-hand man, told everyone.

"Great, just what we needed. Besides the already impossible odds of the ten against ten thousand, now we have to deal with an active volcano. Just perfect," Anvil sarcastically said.

Meanwhile, the captain, Tracks, and their team were still headed north, and just as Tracks had guessed, he soon picked the trail back up, and they followed it until it ended at a small stream. The stream luckily was big enough to be on one of the captain's maps. The map showed the stream running southeast where it eventually met up with a much larger river that turned and ran due south, right to the rendezvous point that Chandler had talked about and to the village of the Manduno people.

Tracks could clearly see impressions on the bank where four large canoes had been taken out of the water and sat for a while. All the fresh tracks came back to the place where the canoes had been at.

Tracks looked at the captain. "Makes sense now why they went north. They were heading back to their rides, the canoes they had left hidden here," Tracks told the captain.

The captain hated it, but he now knew Tab had probably been right. He got out his CB radio and told Chandler that the trail appeared to turn back south and that they would be heading back toward the rendezvous point ASAP. As soon as he got off the radio with Chandler, he turned and told two of his men to get the boats ready.

"We got boats?" Tracks asked jokingly.

CHAPTER 17

Boats

The captain smiled as his men each pulled out a tiny little bag from their backpacks and, at the same time, pulled a small cord attached to each one and toss them on the ground. As soon as the bags hit the ground, they started unfolding while simultaneously airing themselves up, forming two very nice-size rubber rafts.

"Sir, yes sir, we got boats," said the captain, still smiling.

"We should make good time in these toy rafts if the piranhas and the alligators don't eat the bottoms out of them first," Tracks sarcastically replied.

"Sir, it is my opinion that it is better to boat with the gators than it is to walk with the snakes," the captain said, pointing down between Tracks's feet as an eleven-foot green anaconda was slowly slithering between them. Tracks didn't even bother to move. This was the seventh snake today that had been this close to him, and this one between his feet was the first nonpoisonous one of them all.

And with that thought, Tracks smiled and said, "You know maybe a boat ride does sound kind of nice."

Tracks, the captain, and his men loaded their gear onto the large rafts. They pushed the rafts slowly into the water. Tracks, the captain, and one of his men loaded into one raft while the captain's other three men climbed into the second raft. As both rafts got on their way down the stream, Tracks was pleasantly surprised to find out how fast the currents seem to be for such a small stream.

"Wow," Tracks commented, "we're really starting to move. This current is fast it's almost like we got motors on these plastic rafts," Tracks said. Right then, the captain and all his men started bursting out in laughter.

"What is it? What's so funny?" Tracks asked. The captain dried his eyes from laughing so hard and held up a small little remote control. At the same time, one of the captain's men in the other raft did the same thing and held up an exact small little remote control.

"Sir, each raft came with state-of-the-art miniboat motors. They're battery-operated, solar-powered, self-recharging units, and they are both remote-controlled. Gee, Tracks, we're Special Forces. You should know we have all the latest and newest gadgets and toys, sir," the captain told Tracks with a very snide attitude.

Tracks was a little embarrassed by his comments. "I thought this current was moving way too fast," Tracks said under his breath. Everyone heard Tracks's new comment, and it made them all laugh out loud again even harder. Tracks knew he messed up as soon as the words came out of his mouth. Tracks wished he'd picked walking with the snakes now.

CHAPTER 18

Glory Days

Back at the overhang clearing with Chandler and Tab's team, Chandler told everyone that at 1700 hours they would start looking for a place to make camp for the night. Until then, they needed to cover as much ground as they possibility could. But since everyone was already together and stopped, Chandler told everybody to take a thirty-minute break and grab something to eat.

Chandler told everyone that all the backpacks they were wearing were full of good old army rations and to eat up. He also told everybody to plan on not stopping again until it was time to make camp. It was now about 1100 hours, and Chandler was getting hungry himself. It had been a long time since he had eaten army rations. But he was so hungry they were sounding even pretty good to him right now.

As he sat down on an old log to eat, Chandler reminisced about his glory days. He had made quite a name for himself in his younger years as he came up through the ranks of the CIA in almost record speed. For years, he had been one of the best field agents in the department. Chandler's expertise was secret covert missions behind enemy lines. If something needed blowing up or someone needed spied on, then Chandler was your man back in the day.

Being an agent had taken Chandler all around the world; he had been about everywhere. More often than not, his fast thinking and decisive actions kept him safe and slightly ahead of his rivals. He had never been captured or caught in the act in all his years in the field—a record he planned on keeping.

What Chandler needed now was a stiff drink and something to help his sore back, but he knew he would not get either one way out here in the jungle. What he wouldn't give for an hour long massage and a soak in a big, hot bathtub, he thought. Maybe a pretty girl waiting with a towel. Chandler knew he had a better chance of finding Tarzan than he did finding a bottle of good bourbon out in this jungle, but he enjoyed the thought.

Chandler scanned the surrounding jungle and wondered if they were being watched. He knew that everyone's safety ultimately fell on his shoulders, and he knew better than to let his guard down. That's the main reason he always preferred working alone; he only had to watch out for number 1. The best part was not having to share the credit with an entire team when the mission went well. Chandler always did like being the hero.

It saddened him to think that all he's done in the last eight years was just shine a chair with his behind. He had forgotten just how much fun the field was and how profitable it could be. Chandlers age crept up on him as he finally relaxed after he sat down. His back and his legs ached from the day's trek through the jungle. *Oh well,* he thought as he rubbed his sore legs, *this beats a desk job any day of the week.*

CHAPTER 19

Caterpillars

Tab's father Roy, had been talking with the captain's right-hand man, Otto. Seemed Otto was an avid golfer like Roy. Otto was a very interesting fellow, and he and Roy hit it off pretty well. They had a lot in common, especially their love for golf.

Roy looked around and saw Tab sitting next to Bull and Anvil. He walked over to see if she was okay. Bull and Anvil were both eating their rations, but Tab was just sitting there, drinking water out of a vine she had just cut.

"Aren't you hungry, Tab? Why aren't you eating your rations?" her father asked her.

"I'm too full to eat anymore, Dad. I'm just really thirsty right now, and the rations didn't sound very good anyway," Tab answered him.

"What in the world did you eat to fill yourself up on if you didn't eat your rations?" her father asked her.

"I'd tell you, but I don't want to get grounded," Tab told him, giggling.

"You didn't?" her father asked.

Tab shook her head up and down. "Sorry, Dad, but they're everywhere, and they're really delicious. I can't quit eating them. They're like candy. You should try one, Dad. They are almost pure protein. Eat just one, and I promise you will eat a handful," Tab said, trying to convince her father.

The grossed-out look on his face and the way he looked at Tab made Anvil and Bull burst out in laughter. Tab quickly turned and looked over at the two big soldiers.

"No, really guys, they're delicious. You two should try one," Tab told Anvil and Bull.

"I'm with your dad on this one, little girl. It will never happen," Anvil replied. Tab looked over at Bull who was already shaking his head no.

"Sorry honey, but I feel the same way as these two. No way am I eating no bugs," big Bull told Tab.

Tab finally resigned from the discussion smiling. "Oh well, more for me to eat then," Tab told the three of them.

As soon as they all ate, Chandler got the team ready to roll. Everyone took their places back in the line up, and away they went again. Tab and her father both looked up at the sky one last time before the trail again took them deep under the canopy. Once again, Otto and the other three men of the captain's were setting a blistering pace. And once again, as if on cue, here came the rain again.

Tab just happened to glance up as a huge black panther caught her attention. No one else but Tab even saw the big cat. It was just sitting on top of a large branch high up in the canopy following her with its gaze. Tab wasn't scared or afraid, but instead Tab had a strange sense of comfort come over her as she watched the huge beast. Though she did not know the reason for this feeling, she knew it was real. One giant leap and it was gone from her sight, and something told her it would not be the last time she would see this beautiful, magnificent beast.

Tab smiled having seen the Black Panther as it is considered by all who live in the Congo jungle to be very lucky and even a blessing to see one, especially during the daytime. Tab told no one what she saw as she kept pace in the line up following her father through the jungle. Tab couldn't help it, but she found herself looking around occasionally trying to see if she could see it again. There was something about that beautiful beast that she couldn't shake, something about the way it just seemed to be watching her.

CHAPTER 20

Earthquake

Back on the stream with the captain, Tracks, and their team, they had all seen so many alligators that they all stopped bothering to even look anymore. Everyone but Tracks, that is; the alligators were all he could think about as he watched one after the other, from little ones to medium ones to big ones and even a couple of giant ones. It was safe to say that they weren't safe at all in the large rubber rafts.

"I wonder if the gators will get even bigger when we get on bigger water," Tracks asked the captain.

"Sir, after just seeing how big the last one I just saw was, I don't see how they could get any bigger. At least let's hope they don't, Tracks, because it looks like we are getting ready to find out," the captain said, pointing up ahead to where the stream was dumping itself into what appeared to be a much larger and really fast-moving river. Tracks had a really good idea and told the captain to have his men in the other raft to help tie the two rafts together into one long, more stable craft. Tracks's idea seemed even better as they hit the much faster-paced river.

If this pace keeps up, we'll beat Chandler and my buddies to the volcano, Tracks thought to himself. That was if they even make it there as he watched a nineteen-foot alligator swimming alongside them momentarily. It was as long as both the rafts were put together. Tracks sure missed his old Kentucky home as he watched it slowly disappear under the water.

Back with Chandler and Tab's team, they were all still quietly hiking through the jungle. Tab was passing away the time, listening to all the cross talk between everyone when all of a sudden, the jungle came alive above Tab and the rest of her crew. A group of Howler monkeys had not taken them too kindly as the group passed underneath them. They were loud and very angry even after Tab and her team had passed completely by them, they could still be heard angrily screaming off in the distance.

As Tab followed her father Roy, step-by-step through the jungle, her mind wondered to her home back in heaven. How she missed seeing all her family and her Heavenly Father God. She prayed to God that she was doing his will. To be completely honest, she was not exactly sure what God wanted her to do or even where this mission was taking her.

This president Richard Worsham they were all trying to save seemed to be a very good man—extremely proactive about God and religion and he's the first president in a very long time that wanted prayer put back into the schools. Maybe he was the reason God had her out here. She prayed that God would guide her and give her the strength she would need to see this mission to its completion.

She also thanked God for the opportunity he had set before her—a chance to honor him by doing his will down here on earth as she had always tried to do up in heaven. She told God she loved him and that she hoped to see him really soon.

Tab's father interrupted her silent prayer as he turned and asked her if she was doing okay. Tab smiled at him and was just about to answer him when she stopped dead in her tracks. Her father Roy saw her expression change from a happy smile to a look of bewilderment.

"It's happening again! I'm tingling all over again Dad," Tab told her father as she reached out and grabbed his arm and pulled him tightly to her. She yelled into her headset radio, "Everyone, hang on to something! It's going to happen again!" Tab said as she and her father squatted down and held on to each other very tightly. The entire team prepared themselves for the worst.

Suddenly, the ground started to ever so slightly rumble, and then it just quit. Ten seconds later, the team who was still hanging on to trees and to each other started to relax a little bit.

Tab heard Chandler's voice on the radio, "Is that it, Tab? Is that all there is?" he asked.

"I don't think so. I'm still tingling like mad," said Tab, still holding onto her father as if she was going to protect him from something. Chandler waited another fifteen seconds and looked at his watch, still unsure whether it was safe to proceed or not. Just as Chandler was about to call all clear, it hit, and it hit hard.

This earthquake was twice as powerful as the first one was, and it lasted twice as long. The ground appeared to rise and fall a foot as it shook so violently. Several large trees uprooted and fell all around Tab and her team. One tree almost hit Tab and her father, Roy.

Once again, the canopy rained down debris, old limbs, and sticks by the thousands. From over the heads of the captain's four men, an eighteen-foot green anaconda fell down out of the top of the canopy, almost hitting them—it was as scared as they were. Otto looked it right in its eyes and pulled out his very large machete. The snake saw Otto with the big knife, and it didn't want any part of Otto.

Off it went as fast as it could across the jungle floor until it was out of sight. Anvil and Bull found shelter, ducking under a giant rock ledge protruding out from the jungle floor, probably the result from some ancient earthquake similar to the one happening now. Chandler had found refuge in a hollowed-out old tree trunk that was just big enough for him to squeeze into. Suddenly, way off in the distance, a huge ear piercing explosion could be heard.

The ground, which had shook so violently just seconds before, now seemed back to its normal, dorsal state. "I really hope that wasn't the volcano that made that noise," Tab's father, whispered in her ear. He continued holding his daughter very tightly, almost scared to let go of her. Slowly, everyone eased out of their safe havens and looked around.

Otto had dropped all his gear when the earthquake had started. Unfortunately when he finally found his gear, it had been completely smashed by an extremely large tree that had fell nearby. This was the backpack that held the satellite radio in it, so they were now solely on their own and completely cut off from the outside world. Otto hated to tell Chandler, but he called him over and showed him the backpack.

Chandler just shook his head because he knew now that if the president was going to be saved, it would be by them, and them alone doing it. There was not going to be any last-minute reinforcements called in to save the day as that option was now gone.

"At least we still have the fifteen-mile radio, so we can still communicate with Tracks and the captain," Chandler told Otto, trying to make him feel a little better. Otto nodded his head to acknowledge Chandler's attempt, but he still felt responsible.

The destruction caused by the enormous earthquake was massive. They could all see sky above them where only the ceiling of the canopy had been just moments before. And through this huge clearing made by the several extremely large trees that had just fell, everyone could visually confirm what their ears had already told them: the volcano had indeed exploded. The huge explosion had blown away a small portion of the top of the volcano on the north side.

An enormous plume of heavy, thick ash and dark smoke now billowed out of this new, bigger opening at the top of the volcano. Everyone could make out the faint but unmistakable thin red line of hot liquid molten lava coming out and down the north slope of the top of the volcano. The picturesque view was as beautiful as it was deadly.

Moments earlier out on the river, the captain, Tracks, and their team had been making good time with the river current moving so swiftly. Tracks constantly watched the riverbanks, looking at all the alligators and the big bulls that basked out in the sun.

"Hey, look," Tracks yelled suddenly to get everyone's attention. The trees on both sides of the river had started violently shaking. And every gator in sight ran and dove beneath the water of the river, which had now begun to get really choppy as waves crashed over the sides of the rubber rafts.

"Sir, another earthquake," yelled the captain.

"What do we do?" shouted Tracks over the noise of the raging river and the trees as they clashed back and forth.

"Let's try to make it to the riverbank. This water could flip us, sir," yelled the captain at the top of his lungs. Tracks knew that with the piranha and every gator now in the Congo River that ending up in the water was potentially a death sentence.

"Sounds good," Tracks yelled back to the captain. All six men started working the rafts toward the riverbank. Suddenly, as they had almost made it to the bank, a really large tree uprooted and fell into the river. The huge tree landed just twenty yards from them as they tried to make it to the riverbank.

An enormous wave created by the giant girth of the tree nearly capsized both them and their rafts. The giant splash covered all the men in both rafts and completely soaked the men even more than they already were. As soon as their feet hit the bank and they pulled the rafts somewhat out of the water, they heard the huge explosion off in the distance of the top of the volcano blowing apart.

The ground quit shaking almost instantly as the built-up pressure inside the earth was released with the massive explosion of the volcano. From their viewpoint on the edge of the muddy riverbank, they could just make out the top of the giant volcano above the treetops. Immediately after the explosion, every one of them turned in time to view the large ash and smoke plume as it rose over a mile high into the sky.

The captain looked over at Tracks and smiled. "Sir, now we get to get back in the rafts with all the piranhas and all of them big alligators and head towards that," he said, pointing to the smoking volcano.

"Yeah, this trip just keeps getting better. What else can go wrong?" Tracks sarcastically replied. And as if on cue, a large bull alligator took a bite out of the back raft that was still barely hanging over the edge of the river. The big bull alligator pulled both rafts with all their gear back into the river as the damaged raft deflated and shriveled up.

The same big bull alligator then took a bite out of the second raft, sending all their gear except for the backpacks on their backs to the bottom of the river. The most substantial loss was the badly needed fifteen-mile CB radio. It to sank into the river with the rafts.

Everybody turned and looked at Tracks as if he had just caused this whole turn of horrible events.

Tracks looked at everybody looking at him. "Okay, I probably did just jinx us on that. Yeah, for sure, that was my bad. Sorry, sorry, guys," Tracks said, holding his hand up high.

The captain put his hand on Tracks's shoulder. "Sir, at least we weren't in those rafts out on the river when that happened," the captain told Tracks. He looked everybody up and down and continued, "We still have a long way to go, and it looks like we're walking from here on out. Everyone stay alert and stay five meters apart, single line. Let's move out," the captain told everyone. With that being said, they all headed off through the jungle toward the rendezvous point with Chandler and his team.

Back with Chandler and his team, the first thing Chandler thought was why hasn't the captain called him on the CB radio. Chandler grabbed his CB radio and tried to call the captain but got no answer. He tried several more times before he finally gave up. He knew something had happened, but he didn't know what. Knowing there was nothing he could do about it, he knew it was time to get his team moving.

Chandler's team was still in awe, looking at the smoking vol-cano. Chandler got his team's attention and told them that they still had a long way to go and that they needed to get moving. One by one, the captain's four men headed out, taking the lead. Next, Chandler, Tab, and her father Roy followed in behind them while Anvil and Bull once again guarded their flank.

After hiking nonstop for a couple of hours or so, Tab looked at her watch. It was about 1400 hours, and besides several dozen snakes and a run-in with two very large wild hogs, the trek had been a rela-tively drama free one.

Suddenly, across her headset radio, Tab heard, "Chandler, you need to come take a look at this." It was Otto she heard.

"I will be right there, Otto. Everyone else, stay put until I see what's going on," Chandler told everyone. A few minutes later, Tab heard, "Tab, you and Roy, come on up here. I need you to see this," Chandler told them. Tab and her father looked at each other and hurried on up to see what was going on.

CHAPTER 21

The Totem Pole

As Tab and Roy came through some really heavy undergrowth, they saw the captain's men and Chandler all standing in a group. They stood in front of a fifteen-foot tall, very beautifully carved totem pole. It looked as though the area around it had been landscaped, with all the vegetation around the totem pole totally removed. Hung from the totem pole by small ropes made from tiny vines braided together were five old shrunken heads, each not much bigger than a softball.

"What's this mean, Tab?" asked Chandler, pointing to the huge totem pole.

"Actually, totem poles tell many things about the people who made them. Each and every symbol and every carving on them has very specific meanings. This one was made by the Manduno people, and it tells you a lot about their beliefs. It is also a boundary marker, warning and letting everyone know who sees it that they are in the land of the Manduno tribe. The shrunken heads are there to let you know what will happen to you if you do not heed their warning and trespass on their territory. The Manduno tribe have dozens of these encircling their lands. This means we are at the start of their territory."

"What does this one tell us, Tab?" Otto asked.

Tab looked up at the big eagle wings that spread out from the top of the pole and said, "The eagle is worshipped by the Manduno people. They believe it protects them and watches over them from the sky as it soars overhead. Next, there is the carving of the owl symbol below the wings. It represents strength and wisdom. It is against Manduno law to ever harm an owl. They believe their dead ancestors come back as owls to protect and watch over them at night.

"Below the owl is the carving of a black panther. This huge, powerful cat is revered and feared above all the animals of the jungle, even above the mighty gorilla by the Manduno people. They believe the black panther to be a magical beast who rules the nighttime, and to see one in the daytime which is almost never, is a huge blessing to any Manduno who is lucky enough to ever see one. All of the Manduno people worship the black panther as a deity, a living god.

"The next carving is of a thunderbird, a mythical creature with the power to generate lightning and thunder with just the beating of its wings. And last but not least is the carving below the thunderbird. This carving is of Magra, the creature from above the stars and the Manduno tribe's end-of-times creature. I'm sure you all remember me telling you the story of him earlier back at base camp.

"It is on all of their totem poles, and it is always at the bottom to signify the end of their people. They say that knowing they will all someday die at the coming of this creature makes them fearless in the face of battle—why fear death when it surely comes for them anyway? To the Manduno people, to die in war is just a chance to cheat Magra out of one of his victims," Tab told everybody as they listened, totally engrossed in her story of the totem pole.

"Wow, Tab, all of that is represented on that pole. That is amazing," Otto said. Chandler looked at Otto to get his attention and then turned and faced the team.

"We are now getting ready to enter the Manduno territory, and you will all need to stay focused and get your heads back in the game. This mission just got real, so let's just forget about the totem pole, and everyone take five to check your gear and your weapons. Lock and load'em, gentleman. This isn't a drill. We are in the middle of no man's land in hostile territory, and we have a job to do. Let's stay focused and just get to the rendezvous point as quickly and silently as possible.

Tab interrupted Chandler just as the rain came pouring down again. "Sir, the Manduno warriors patrol their land vigorously. The closer we get to their village, the higher the chance for us to have a run in with them. And they always travel in groups of ten or more. The fact that they greatly outnumber us is not the issue at hand here. The issue is if they think we are coming to take their royal prisoner from them, they may possibly go ahead and take his life and his head," Tab told Chandler.

"What are you suggesting we do, Tab?" Chandler asked.

CHAPTER 22

Sacred Burial Ground

"There is a stretch of land close to here that the Manduno people use to put their dead to rest in. It is their sacred burial ground. Only tribal witch doctors may enter this sacred area. It is believed by the Manduno people that if anybody else other than a witch doctor were to enter this sacred land that they would forever be cursed and die a painful, horrible death. No Manduno warrior would ever dare to enter that land for any reason, but we could still be seen as we cross it.

"I know of an old, abandoned small Aztec-style pyramid in that area that we could hold up in until it gets dark. Then using our night vision goggles, we could travel throughout the night to our meeting spot with Tracks and the captain. Then all we have to do is hide out until they get to us. And even though the Manduno do go on missions at night, they never patrol after dark, so the chances of a run in with them would be very slim," Tab told Chandler.

Chandler thought for a few moments, pondering all that Tab had told him. He knew traveling through the jungle in the dark could be very dangerous in itself. But if Tab was correct and the Manduno would kill the president if they were discovered, then what choice did he really have? With the heat and night vision goggles they all had, it might just be the safest way to travel to the rendezvous point. He knew the Manduno did not have any equipment at all, and with no moonlight coming down through the canopy, his team would be virtually invisible to everyone.

"Tab, you just might be a genius. Otto take Tab and Roy up to the front with you so Tab can show us the way to the sacred burial grounds and to the pyramid she was talking about. This may just work," Chandler told everybody. Chandler was also thinking to himself just how much he wanted to see this pyramid.

Tab was now basically leading the way. And it wasn't long before Tab and her team had made it to the sacred burial ground of the Manduno people. A small two-foot ancient-looking wall had been built around the entire sacred area. It disappeared in both directions like a miniature Great Wall of China. Tab wasted no time trying to explain the wall, and she just stepped over it and continued on. Everybody behind her followed suit, and soon they were all over it and going deeper into the sacred burial ground. The team was now traveling as quietly as possible and just a few feet apart from each other. They stayed low to the ground and moved as quickly as they could.

It didn't take them long to start coming across burial stands, seven to eight-foot-high platforms built up off the ground to hold the bodies of the Manduno dead. The closer they got to their destination, the more stands they came across until almost all you could see was rows and rows of platforms. It was truly a cold chills up your spine, eerie scary kind of sight.

Finally, Tab led the team to the entranceway of the pyramid. The entranceway consisted of two very large free standing columns. They were both precision-cut rectangular stones, and each stood ten foot tall and were about three by three square foot. They were so smooth they looked like they had been cut yesterday, but they were no doubt centuries old.

From these stones, they could all see a small trail leading up to the small, ancient Aztec-style pyramid. From the ground, it staircased up on all sides, getting more triangular-shaped the higher it got. The rocks going up were all completely covered by grass and weeds. The very top appeared to be flat, and they could all see what looked like a large table made from cut rock up there. A sacrificial table, they all guessed. It was a very impressive sight to say the least.

The path leading up to the pyramid was laid in perfectly square cut rock. Though mostly covered in grass and weeds, the rocks could still clearly be seen. Looking at the pyramid, a large entranceway opening could be seen facing the two large stones. As Tab and her team moved away from the two large stones and walked closer toward the pyramid entrance, they could all easily see it had been abandoned a very long time ago.

The opening was almost completely grown over and sealed shut by vines, brush, and weeds. Chandler told Otto to use his machete to cut an opening in it but just big enough for everyone to fit through it. Otto made quick work of it with his machete and cut a perfect-size hole in the vines. Otto then grabbed three large green bend and shake light sticks out of his backpack. After bending and shaking each one, Otto threw them into the darkness of the hole he had just made in the vines. A green glow slowly lit up the darkness, and Otto cautiously stuck his head through the opening to have a look.

"You guys have got to see this," Otto told everyone as he pulled his head out.

"Why what is it?" Chandler asked.

"Take a look for yourself," Otto told him. Chandler stepped up and slowly stuck his head into the opening. He immediately stepped on into the opening of the pyramid and then stuck his hand back out to motion everyone to come on in.

One by one, everyone stepped through the small opening in the vines and into the pyramid. Bull had a little trouble as big as he was, but he managed to force his way on in. As everyone began lighting their own light sticks, Bull stood up from crawling through the opening and was momentarily blinded by a white light. He looked over to see Tab outlined in a brilliant glowing light. As quickly as he saw it, it faded and was gone. Bull quickly looked at everybody's face, and he could tell that he had been the only one that was able to see the light around Tab.

"You need a light, Bull? I got one," Tab asked Bull as he walked toward her.

"Yeah, I saw that," Bull answered her.

"What do you mean, Bull?" Tab said after she saw the weird look on Bull's face.

"Oh, nothing, just trying to be funny, Tab," Bull told Tab. Bull thought maybe he should just keep what he saw to himself, at least for now. Everyone could already see in the dimly lit green glow of the first light sticks that Otto had thrown in. But now that everyone else's light sticks had began lighting up, everyone could easily see the inside of the large room they stood in. Seven large golden-looking discs hung on the walls, evenly spaced around the room. Little rock ledges jutted out from the walls under each one to help hold them up. Between every disc was an old torch bracket, a wooden torch still hung in each one of them. The room was very large, and it was built in the form of a circle.

At the opposite end of the room was a very beautifully carved wooden throne. You could just picture a tribal king sitting in it. What jumped out at Chandler were the rubies and emeralds that ran up and down the chair, from the top down both sides out to each armrest. But even they didn't compare to the massive diamond sitting at the top of the chair.

It was the biggest diamond Chandler had ever seen. They were all so perfectly inlaid in the wood that it looked like a jeweler from today had done the work. On each side of the throne chair was an old torch bracket with a wooden torch in one of them. Whatever whoever used to do in this room, the room still looked ready to do it again, minus a good cobweb cleaning.

After everyone had made it inside the pyramid and admired all there was to admire, Chandler looked around and nodded his head.

"Tab, this should do just fine," he told her. Chandler looked down at his watch and continued, "It is approximately 1700 hours right now. We'll head back out at 2100 hours. That should be enough time for us all to get some much-needed rest and hopefully late enough for the Manduno tribe to be in for the night. So, everybody, grab some wall and try to get some sleep," Chandler told everyone. Chandler then turned to Otto and the captain's other men, "Secure the hole in the vines with some rope. That's the only way in or out of here. Then you four get some rest yourselves. I don't think it will be necessary to stand watch tonight," Chandler told Otto.

"Yes, sir," Otto answered back, happy to hear what Chandler had said.

Two of the captain's men gathered some rope and started securing the opening for the night. Chandler walked over to Otto, "Any contact from Tracks or Captain Butler yet?" Chandler asked Otto.

"No, sir, still no word from either of them, and I am getting a little concerned, sir," Otto told Chandler.

"Yeah, me too, Otto. Last contact I had with them had them on their way to the rendezvous point. Let's hope they are there when we get there," Chandler said with a worried look on his face. Otto nodded his head and hoped Chandler was right. Maybe they were just having radio problems, he thought to himself.

"Do you want me to keep trying them?" Otto asked Chandler.

"Get some rest first. I need you fresh when we head out later. We'll try them again before we head out," Chandler told him.

"Yes, sir," Otto answered.

Thirty minutes earlier, with the captain, tracks, and their team, they had all been looking for a safe place to bed down for the night. But they were not having a lot of luck in finding a safe accommodation for the night. It had just started pouring down rain again, and their moral had gotten really low. They were just about to give up when the unexpected happened.

CHAPTER 23

Crash-Landing

Tracks came across an old cargo plane that had crash-landed through the canopy decades ago. They all practically ran over to it to investigate it. From the looks of it, the men guessed it was an old 1950s cargo plane. The captain and copilot must have been killed instantly. They were still in the cockpit and still in their company's uniforms, but they were nothing but bones.

Insects had completely done the job the Good Lord God had put them on the earth to do. Lucky for Tracks, the captain, and his men, they now all had a safe place to try and get some sleep. The plane's door still opened and closed, and it even still locked. Tracks had not been looking forward to sleeping out in the open. He was so thankful he dropped to his knees and openly thanked God for helping them find the downed plane. The captain and of his men were equally as thankful, and each man said, "Amen" when Tracks finished thanking God.

After all six men investigated the aircraft inside and out, they each started settling down and finally began to relax for a moment. Having a door that they could lock sure made it easier to unwind. One by one, they each started yawning and getting more and more comfortable. Tracks took off his boots and rubbed his aching feet. Soon, all the men had taken off their boots and began stretching out up and down the cargo bay.

The men didn't bother to talk much as they were all extremely worn-out from the day's adventures. Within thirty minutes, every one of them was out cold and snoring. It was hard to see how any of them could sleep at all as loud as they all were.

CHAPTER 24

Treasures

Back in the pyramid with Chandler, Tab, and their team. As Tab and the men settled in to try and get some sleep, Chandler walked over to the nearest disc on the wall to inspect it, and just as he thought, it was pure gold. He hated the thought, but he knew he would have to leave the disc and all the jewels for now. They've no doubt been safely hidden here in this pyramid for who knows how long. *Another week or two shouldn't hurt anything*, he thought to himself.

He knew Tab would be his ticket to millions of dollars, but this one room alone came to more than all his earlier fantasies combined. "Hello, retirement," Chandler whispered to himself as he slid down the wall to try and get some sleep himself.

An alarm went off and then another one. Slowly, everybody started to wake up. Chandler and Otto had both set their watch alarms. The day's hike had apparently gotten to all of them as every single one of them had been out cold and sound asleep. The light sticks that everybody had lit earlier were now barely glowing. Otto started to snap light another one, but Chandler stopped him.

"No lights of any kind, night vision goggles only from here on out," he reminded everybody. Roy helped Tab put hers on and showed her how to turn them off and on.

"Thanks, Dad," Tab said as she leaned over and kissed his cheek.

"That's what I'm here for: to help my baby girl," Roy said, smiling. Now his face turned more serious. "Tab, if something happens to me, I want you to know how much I love you. And how proud and happy I am that God made you my daughter this time around. Promise me you'll take care of your mother. Without me, she may seem a bit lost for a little while. Lord knows I would if something were to ever happen to her. Tab, she'll need you more than ever," Her father told her as Tab interrupted. "Dad, please don't talk that way," she said as she leaned into her father and hugged him very tightly. "Let's both just pray to God that by his will, we will both make it through all of this," Tab continued.

"Can I get in on this prayer?" Bull very softly asked.

Then everyone started asking to be included in the prayer. Chandler asked Tab to stand, and he reached out his own hands in both directions. Slowly, everybody formed a huge circle and grabbed the hands of the person next to them. As soon as the circle was complete, Tab bowed her head and waited a few seconds for everyone to do the same, and then she began.

"Dear, Heavenly Father, we come to you in this our time of need. We pray, dear Father, that you will guide us on this mission. Please watch over and protect each one of us. By holding hands, we hope to show you how united we stand in this effort to go forth to do your will, my heavenly Father. We know and appreciate everything you have done for us, and we thank you for this chance to honor you. By the blood of your son, Jesus Christ, our Savior, we ask this of you in his name. Amen," Tab said with her eyes still closed.

Everyone, still holding hands, silently said, "Amen."

Chandler then looked up and said, "Let's move out."

It almost killed Chandler to leave all the treasures behind, but he knew he had to get everybody moving. He wanted to get to the rendezvous spot before it got daylight. Otto and Chandler tried the captain on the CB radio one more time before they left, but they still had no luck reaching him. They both were worried, but both still hoped for the best. Maybe they would be there in the morning waiting on them.

As his team, one by one, crawled out of the ancient little pyramid into the darkness, Chandler stood at the opening in the vines and took one last look back into the green-tinted dimly lit room. He looked at the jewels in the throne chair and then at the seven large golden discs barely visible hanging on the walls. Chandler had to make his self turn away. He then wondered what other treasures Tab might lead them all too in this adventure they were on. This thought gave him the strength he needed to leave the pyramid and his treasures behind.

CHAPTER 25

The Jungle at Night

As Chandler's team headed out into the darkness of the jungle, the military-grade night vision goggles worked as planned. The team was virtually invisible as they silently maneuvered through the sacred burial grounds. Each member of the team was able to see a good sixty to seventy feet in front of them. It was like walking in daylight with green-tinted sunglasses.

The only bad thing was that the green tint of the night vision goggles made all the burial platforms they passed look even that much more eerie and scary. The jungle all by itself can be an eerie place at nighttime. All the nocturnal predators, snakes and big cats, use the darkness to hunt and ambush prey in. The noise alone at night is enough to frighten someone to death.

All the far-off growls, animal squeals, and things running and crashing through the jungle in every direction is enough to give someone a heart attack—that, along with all the flying insects buzzing and all the crickets chirping combined with every frog in the jungle singing their romantic ballads. As bizarre as it may sound but the jungle was at least twice as loud at night as it was during the daytime.

Something else that was far worse in the nighttime was the mosquitoes. Walls of them came at you. If it wasn't for the team's full-body gear and the bug spray they each heavily sprayed constantly all over their body and heads, they'd all been eaten alive. And then there were all the other flying and biting insects at night.

Not to even mention the infamous vampire bats that flew around the jungle at night. Tab hoped the team didn't run into any of them that night. She has had her share of vampire bat encounters, and if she lived another forty lives here in this jungle and never seen one again, that would be just fine with her.

Tab was once again leading the way through the sacred burial ground. It was now about 2200 hours, and they were still approximately four hours away from the rendezvous point. But everyone had gotten some much-needed rest, and the team felt strong and refreshed. Maybe it was the adrenaline of the nighttime or the cooler temperature of the night air, but Tab was setting a pretty impressive pace herself.

Tab was following an old trail through the burial platforms, one probably used to bring in the dead. Tab had just come down a small embankment when the trail suddenly opened up and split off in three different directions, sort of like a four-way intersection. Tab told everyone to take a small break so she could take a moment to figure out the best path for them to take.

One by one, everyone came into the clearing and sat down. Tab walked up to each of the two paths going ninety degrees from the one they had been on and looked down them as far as her goggles allowed her to. As she turned and walked toward the third trail, the one that lined up with the one they had been on, a huge black panther leapt out in front of Tab, blocking her path. The two stood motionless and just stared at each other.

CHAPTER 26

Shadow

The huge, powerful cat did not growl at Tab nor did it show any signs of aggression. It just stood there and stared at her. Tab's father Roy looked over at Tab to see what she was doing, and he saw the big cat. He immediately leapt to his feet and pulled his pistol.

Tab was standing between him and the panther. Roy told Tab as quietly as he was able, trying not to spook the big cat, to very slowly move out of his way so he could shoot it. Now everyone was on their feet with their guns drawn. Tab put her hand up in the air and told everyone very sternly to stand down and to not shoot the panther.

Tab was staring deep into the eyes of the black panther. She slowly took one step forward, and still, the huge beast's gaze never left her own. Tab's father could hardly contain himself, and as quietly as he could yell, her father asked her, "Tab, what are you doing, girl? Have you lost your mind?" Tab again put her hand up as she took yet another step toward the panther. She could sense it would not harm her, and she was now only four feet from the enormous black cat. Suddenly, inside of Tab's head, she could hear the black panther's heart beating. It was a calm and relaxed heartbeat, not one of hidden aggression. Everyone held their breath as they watched Tab so close to the wild black panther.

Tab smiled and stuck out her hand as one would when approaching a large canine. The huge panther which had been locking eyes with Tab cautiously dropped its gaze to her outstretched hand. It moved forward ever so slowly, placing its massive head under her small hand. Tab started rubbing its head and face as it started purring like a big house cat.

Tab knelt down, and it snuggled its huge neck up against hers. The second Tab snuggled her head back up against the panthers, she was instantly jolted with all the panther's knowledge and the reason why it leapt out at her. Tab continued to rub and scratch her new friend as their minds melted into each others. Her father Roy, and everyone else were speechless at what had just unfolded in front of them.

Big Bull, who was standing next to Roy, nudged him. "I haven't told anyone this, but back in the pyramid before we all lit it up real good, I looked over at Tab, and she was outlined in a brilliant white light," Bull whispered to Roy.

Roy looked up at Bull with a puzzled look. "Outlined in white light?" he asked.

"Yes, sir, completely in brilliant white light. It was like she was glowing or something. And now this, I'm telling you, sir. She has God in her. I just know it," Bull said confidently.

Roy looked at Bull and nodded his head in agreement with everything Bull had just said.

"Tab," Chandler quietly said as he tried to get her attention without startling the panther.

Tab looked over at Chandler. "He's a friend, and he won't harm any of us. It only leapt out at me to warn me of a pitfall trap down that trail," Tab told Chandler as she pointed down the trail going straight ahead. "He's been following us this whole time, and he thought I was going to go on down that trail, and he was afraid for me," Tab continued. Everybody looked at each other in disbelief at what Tab had just told them.

Bull leaned in close to Roy and nudged him again. "I told you so. You can't talk to animals without God in you," big Bull whispered again to Roy.

Chandler, with a disbelieving look on his face, asked Tab, "It told you all of that?"

"Actually, it never spoke to me. I do not speak panther," Tab said as she laughed trying to ease the moment with a little laughter.

No one was laughing though as everyone was still in total disbelief. "I kind of read its mind is the best answer I have to explain this. Shadow said there are several more pitfall traps along the trails from here to the Manduno village. He said he would lead us around all of them," Tab told Chandler and everybody.

Chandler looked over at Tab, and with a new dumbfounded look on his face, Chandler asked, "Shadow, your new friend's name is Shadow?"

Tab confessed, "I sort of just named him Shadow, but he likes it. Sorry, but I always wanted a black cat named Shadow," Tab said, trying to justify her actions.

Bull walked over toward Tab and Shadow. "Can I pet Shadow?" he asked Tab.

"Sure, Bull. He won't bite you. He's here to help us," Tab answered Bull. Bull walked right up to the massive black panther and started petting and rubbing his thick dark fur. Shadow purred like a big house cat. Slowly, everyone came over and petted the huge beast, even Chandler.

Tab's father Roy, went over and gave Tab a big hug. "You're amazing, baby girl," her father whispered.

"It's not me, Dad. It's our Heavenly Father working through me. All the glory is his. I am just proud to be a part of it all," Tab replied. Hearing this humble statement from his daughter made him hug her even tighter.

"I love you, Tab," he whispered again.

"I love you too, dad," she replied.

Chandler took his turn to pet Shadow just like everyone else did. He was so amazed at Tab and all her gifts.

Chandler knew it was time he got his team up and moving. "Okay, everybody, we need to get going," He told everyone. Hearing Chandler's statement, Shadow stood up and walked off down the path that headed to the left.

"I guess he heard you," Anvil said to Chandler.

"Follow Shadow," Tab told everybody. Tab rushed up and fell in behind Shadow. The team now led by Shadow, marched two solid hours through the darkness without incident until Shadow abruptly stopped. Tab walked up to Shadow and leaned down, putting her arm around the big cat's neck. Tab stayed like that for a couple of minutes then stood up and turned back toward everybody. "Shadow says there's danger up ahead. There is a pitfall trap just about ten yards up in this trail we're on," Tab told everyone silently through her headset radio. Shadow said we need to go around it.

"Why do the Manduno people have pitfall traps on their burial trails?" Chandler asked Tab.

"I asked Shadow that very question, and he said that other white men in the past had come to pillage the burial platforms. Shadow said this was just one of the many ways the Manduno try to deter unwanted visitors. It is a well-known fact that all the tribes throughout the Congo Basin send rubies, emeralds, and sometimes even gold with their dead loved ones for their trip to the land of the dead."

Tab told everyone then added from her own personal knowledge of her time spent here in the Congo, "I guess word got out, and greed finally got involved. The Manduno must have had no choice but to finally add these booby traps to try and protect their dead loved ones' possessions," Tab said with a sad look on her face.

Chandler looked down the trail. It looked as normal as any other part of the trail. *The Manduno must be as good at camouflage as Tab had said*, Chandler thought.

"Tell Shadow thanks from all of us. No way we would have seen that without his help. I can't even see it now," Chandler told Tab. Tab nodded that she would do as Chandler had asked her. With one giant leap, the big cat Shadow was over the pitfall and back on good trail waiting for them.

He waited while everyone else had to walk around through the thick brush, cutting and climbing their way through every thorny inch of it. After they were all safely back on the trail, Chandler had Otto find the pitfall. He wanted a better look at it to see what kind of people they were going up against. Otto used his razor-sharp machete to cut himself a long eight-foot stick that he used to slowly poke at the ground. After several pokes at the ground, sure enough, the stick suddenly sank right into it.

Otto signaled to Chandler that he had found it. Both Otto and Chandler laid down on their stomachs and peered down into the pitfall. The pitfall trap was a good ten feet deep, as wide as the trail and eight foot long. A dozen or more one-inch-round sharpened sticks rose up from the floor of the trap waiting to pierce any unsuspecting quest that fell through for a visit.

Chandler and Otto stood back up. Chandler looked back down at the top of the pitfall trap, and even up as close as he was, he could not tell it was there. Maybe it was the green tint that he was seeing it in, but the top had been made by a true camouflage expert.

Once again, Shadow took the lead. They came to several more trail intersections, but Shadow never even hesitated. He just headed this way or that way, apparently very confident of where he was leading everybody. Several times along the way, he put his extremely large tail up in Tab's face, playing with her.

Tab's father Roy, was following closely behind her and watched how Tab and Shadow were playing back and forth. He felt so much better knowing this big, mighty cat was going to be protecting his daughter. Roy started praying silently to himself as he followed his daughter Tab. He thanked the Lord for all his blessings and, oddly enough, for allowing him the honor of being Tab's father.

He assured God that he would go all out to help his daughter Tab carry out his will. He praised the good Lord many times for all the help that he knew God had sent their way. He asked God to please watch over his beloved wife back home and to comfort her worries while they were away. Roy finished the prayer with a very heart felt amen.

The team started to smell smoke and ash from the volcano the closer they got to it. They had been traveling for about four hours now. The temperature seemed way too high for it to be night time. Maybe it was the pace Shadow had been setting, but it was hot. So everyone was so thankful when it finally started pouring down rain again. Well, everyone except Shadow, that is. It was very obvious he was not happy. But he stayed committed and kept leading the team.

CHAPTER 27

The Rendezvous Point

Chandler's night vision goggles had been starting to fade in and out. He spoke softly and asked everybody through his headset radio if any of them had been having the same trouble with their goggles. Both Otto and Anvil said they had been having the very same issue with theirs.

Chandler told Tab that as soon as there was a break in the rain for her to please find a place, they could all take a quick break. Mainly so everyone could change out the batteries in their night vision goggles. Chandler knew they were getting close to the Manduno village, and he did not want any vision issues should a fight break out.

"Next clearing we come to after the rain stops, I'll pull over if that's okay," Tab said, almost giggling.

"That will do just fine," answered Chandler.

Twenty minutes later, they were all stopped and changing out their batteries. Shadow was nearly sitting in Tab's lap as Tab scratched and loved all over her big furry friend. Roy changed out Tab's batteries and then his own; he even changed out Chandler's.

Otto and his three men stood at the ready until everyone else had all changed out their batteries. Then Bull and Anvil stood guard until the four soldiers had each changed out theirs. Finally, every one of them had good, strong night vision goggles to finish out their midnight trek through the jungle.

The smoke from the volcano had started to get thick and heavy. Off in the distance, the orange glow of fire could clearly be seen. The faint but unmistakable sound of drums could also be heard.

Chandler and Otto came over to Tab and asked her how much farther until they arrived at the rendezvous point. Tab told them they were getting really close, maybe thirty to forty-five minutes more depending on how good the trail stayed.

Chandler then asked Tab if she was still sure she knew of a place they could all hide out in until Tracks and the captain showed up and, more importantly, could she find it in the dark. Tab said yes to both questions. She said there was a giant boulder right along the riverbank that no one could miss and that it was right at a point where a small stream joined the main river. Tab said there was an old trail that led to up the volcano to several small caves that overlooked the river. Tab said she knew exactly the one that everybody could hide in.

A thought came to Otto, and he told it to Chandler, "Depending on the distance, our headset radios are identical to the captain's and his teams. We should be able to communicate with them as soon as they come into range," Otto excitedly told Chandler.

"Good thinking, Otto. That is great news," Chandler replied to Otto. Then Chandler had a thought, and he told Otto, "They're all probably sound asleep right now. They did not know they needed to travel at night." He looked down at his watch. "I'd say the earliest we could expect them would be 1200 hours, maybe an hour either way," Chandler said.

"And I'd say that's probably a pretty close estimate, sir, by my calculations as well. But if they are not here by 1300 hours at the latest, I think we have no choice but to roll without them. Maybe something bad happened to them after that last earthquake," Otto hated to say it, but he did.

"I agree that if they are still a no-show at 1300 hours, then we will have no choice but to roll without them. I hope they make it here or at least call us on the CB radio. It would be nice to know they were safe and even nicer to have them with us because we could sure use their help," Chandler told Otto as he nodded his head in agreement. Tab heard the conversation and started praying to God for their friends' safe return.

The team headed back out cautiously. As close as they were, Chandler told everyone to move with purpose, slow and silent, from here on out. Shadow and Tab led the team down toward the river, and they traveled parallel to it. Not so close that the gators could get at the team. But close enough to hide them in the heavy growth from wandering eyes as Tab and her team traveled closer to the volcano and the Manduno village.

Drums, screaming, and chanting could be heard over the normal noise of the jungle. It sounded like the Mandunos were throwing a party. As they continued closer, Chandler softly asked Tab through the headset radio if she knew what was happening.

"They are throwing Mantoro, the volcano god they worship, a celebration. They hope to appease his anger. These events usually last for several days, so I'd say the president is still safe for now. But I know the warriors will be out looking for sacrifices. It will not be a good day for anybody they find out in the jungle during one of these events," Tab replied.

After hearing this last comment from Tab, everyone on the team started really worrying about Tracks, the captain, and his other four men. Her comment even made her start to worry, and for a little while, they all walked in silence, each silently prayed in their own way that the other team would find safe passage to them.

Finally, the team came upon a large boulder just like Tab said they would, right across from where a small stream joined with the main river. A small overgrown trail led the team up the volcano to the first of several small caves. Tab passed up the first two, and after removing some brush growing around the third cave, Tab led the team into it. The inside of the cave was dry and actually quite roomy. It had two tunnels that led out from the main room.

After everyone had entered the cave, they formed a small circle as Tab gave intel about the cave and tunnels. "This tunnel dead-ends only a few hundred yards into the volcano," Tab said, pointing down the first tunnel. "The other tunnel is the one that leads to two secret chambers that The Manduno use to incarcerate and prepare victims for sacrifice, usually to Mantoro, their volcano god. Down this tunnel is where they should be holding the president.

It's a long journey through the tunnels, and with the volcano acting up, I don't know how safe a journey it will be. But it's got to be a safer bet than fighting the Manduno to get him back. Chandler took in all that Tab had told him. As far as he was concerned, they would stick to the original plan until they could no longer do so.

After Tab was done giving details of the two tunnels that left the cave, no one said a word as they looked around and investigated the inside of the cave. Maybe it was due to sheer exhaustion or the fear of being discovered, but hardly a word was muttered from anyone.

Chandler looked down at his watch. "Everybody may as well get comfortable and try to get some sleep. We are going to be here for a quite some time, and I need everyone fresh and on their game come daybreak," Chandler told everyone.

"Shadow has offered to stand guard so we all can get some sleep, and he says he hears everything for us not to worry," Tab told Chandler.

Chandler looked over at Shadow. "Thanks, Shadow, I was just getting ready to set guard," Chandler told the big cat.

Shadow nodded his big furry head in acknowledgement of Chandler's gratitude.

Otto came over to Chandler. "Set our alarms for ten hundred hours sound about right to you, sir?" Otto asked Chandler.

"Sounds good to me, Otto," Chandler replied back. Both Chandler and Otto raised their arms at the same time to set their watch alarms. Slowly, everyone settled down. They leaned back against the cave walls and, one by one, turned off their night vision goggles.

Tab's father Roy, whispered in the dark, "I love you, Tab. Try to get some sleep. I am exhausted, and I bet you are too."

Tab reached out in the darkness and found her father's hand and gave it a good squeeze. "I love you too, dad. Get some sleep, I am okay," she told her father.

After the teams all-night hike, it didn't take long before Tab and Shadow were the only two awake. Tab leaned up against Shadow like he was a big furry pillow. Tab had no worries as she laid snuggled up against the mighty beast. Its huge chest and stomach rose and fell with it's every breath. Almost hypnotically, it began to softly rock her to sleep. Tab barely finished her nightly prayers before she to was fast asleep.

CHAPTER 28

Quicksand

While Tab and the others slept hidden in their cave, several hours away, a loud bang to the top of the cargo plane abruptly woke up the captain, tracks, and their entire team. The captain and Tracks looked at each other at the same time. The captain put his finger to his mouth and motioned for everyone to stay silent. Tracks looked at the captain and shrugged his shoulders, letting the captain know he didn't have a clue as to just what made that noise.

Looking outside the plane's window, they could all see it was light outside. Tracks looked down to check his watch when suddenly scurrying little footsteps could be heard on the roof of the plane. One of the captain's men who was still lying quietly on the floor where he had slept looked up and out the window and saw a small, wide-eyed little spider monkey staring right back at him.

"Captain, it's little monkeys making all the noise up on the roof," he said, almost whispering. Tracks held his wrist watch up and got the captain's attention.

He pointed to his watch. "We better be heading out, sir. It's getting late," Tracks told the captain. The captain looked down and checked his own watch. He stood right up and grabbed his shirt and his gear.

"Time to go gentlemen," he said. Ten minutes and several mad spider monkeys later, everybody was dressed and standing outside the plane.

"I thought we were in a rainforest, but I am about to freeze to death," Tracks said, shivering.

"Yes, sir, it is cool, but I like this better than the heat. I think I saw a thin jacket in my backpack. Maybe you got one too, sir," the captain told Tracks. While everybody dug in their backpacks looking for something warm to put on, the captain started talking, "With the time we made up on the river, I'd say we should be about here," he said, pointing to a small map he had pulled out from his backpack. "We know this river runs right into the rendezvous point with Chandler and his team, so I say we just follow it and try to stay out of sight," the captain told everyone.

"How far away do you think we still are?" Tracks asked the captain.

"Sir, I am guessing we are still about four or five hours away," the captain replied.

"I say we try and make it in three, and I'll take the lead," Tracks said. And with that, he turned and headed off paralleling the river with everyone staying tight and hot on his heels. Tracks and his team were about an hour from the old cargo plane following an old game trail. Tracks had been setting a blistering pace when on his next leap from a fallen tree, he landed waist-deep in quicksand.

The captain had just momentarily stopped to tighten a strap on his backpack when he looked up just in time to see Tracks jump and disappear. The captain started laughing to himself because he thought Tracks had fallen when he landed because he never rose back up. But after a few seconds when he didn't reappear, the captain knew something was wrong and rushed over and stood on the same log Tracks had leapt from and looked down.

The captain could see the panic on Tracks's face. Tracks had began to slowly but steadily sink deeper and deeper into the quicksand. He was almost up to his belly button, and the more he moved, the faster he sank. The captain told Tracks not to panic and to stay still. He told him he was about to teach him a handy little survival skill for situations just like the one he was in.

"Forget the lesson. Just get me out of here please," Tracks said in a panic.

"In due time, sir," said the captain. He then turned to one of his man standing directly behind him who just so happened carried a big machete and asked him to quickly cut down a two or three-inch-round small tree several feet long. They were everywhere, and a few moments later, the captain had one in his hand. He reached out as far as he could and handed it to Tracks.

"What do I do with this? Just throw me a rope," Tracks said in a panic.

"Sir, we'll never be able to pull you out like that as deep as you are. Now shut up and do exactly as I say, and I'll have you out of there in a minute or two," the captain said very sternly.

Tracks nodded his head up and down and felt a little calmer with all the confidence the captain was showing.

"Lay the limb at your waist, sir, and simply bend over it as far as you can. Use your arms and stomach muscles and slowly pull your legs back and up through the mud, not out of the mud. Try to think of it as straightening your body out flat on top of the mud using the stick to pivot your center on, sir," the Captain told him all this while simultaneously acting out what he wanted Tracks to do.

Tracks watched the captain closely and did as he was instructed to do. And in a couple of minutes, he had managed to pull his legs up and out through the quicksand. Tracks was now laid out flat across the stick. "Now what do I do?" Tracks asked the captain.

"Just stay as flat as you can and army crawl across the surface of the quicksand, sir," said the captain. Once again, Tracks did as he was told, and soon he was standing on the edge of the quicksand, worn-out but happy to be out and alive.

The quicksand mud had the consistency of tar and was as hard to clean off. After cleaning himself off the best he could, Tracks walked over to the captain and thanked him for saving his life. The captain could see how fatigued Tracks had made himself fighting his way out of the quicksand. The captain told everybody to take five to allow Tracks time to gather himself.

While Tracks rested his nerves as much as his body, the Captain pulled out his maps and went over the best route to get to the rendezvous point. Following the river still seemed the fastest and best plan. Several minutes later, they were all up and following the same game trail they had been on earlier. Tracks took the lead again, only this time he carried with him the same long stick that saved his life. He didn't want to ever be caught in that situation again, especially without his stick.

One good thing about this morning's hike was the temperature. It felt even cooler than it was this morning when they all woke up. It felt a good twenty-five to thirty degrees cooler than it was the day before. And the humidity was way down also, very unusual weather for the Congo Basin, unusual but very welcomed.

Another thing that the entire team had started noticing was a faint burning smell. It seemed to get stronger the closer they ventured toward the volcano. Each of them wondered as they trekked through the jungle just what they were heading into.

Would the area be burnt to the ground? Would the Manduno people evacuate their village because of the volcano and be gone when they got there? If so, then where would the president be and how would they ever find where they took him? So many unanswered variables. Every one of these soldiers normally worked like finely tuned surgeons. They always had access to the latest, best intel. They would make their incision, go in, and cut and take out whatever they needed to fast and in a hurry and usually be gone and back at their base camp on a tightly knit schedule.

This was all very new to each of them, this wandering around through the jungle not knowing any intel about almost anything. Something more then just duty was compelling them all, and they all knew it. Almost every one of them would have pulled the plug on this mission any other time. But some force much greater than themselves drove them on into the unknown of whatever laid ahead.

Tracks found himself constantly looking where he was stepping instead of what laid ahead. He couldn't get the quicksand out of his mind. In all his years out in the woods, he had never had a run in with the stuff. It didn't even exist back in the mountains of eastern Kentucky where he came from. If it hadn't been for the captain's experience, he'd been a gonner for sure, Tracks thought to himself.

Tracks knew one thing: he'd never be in the woods or in a jungle again without his new big stick or one like it. No way was he ever going to feel that helpless again if he had anything to say about it. Tracks could still feel the sensation of how he slowly began to sank into the quicksand and he thought of all the people who may have died that way. The thought sent shivers up and down his spine.

CHAPTER 29

The Green Mamba

The captain, tracks, and their team had been making good time. The captain looked down at his watch and saw it was a few minutes before ten hundred hours. The captain was following tight on the heels of Tracks, who was still setting a blistering pace. The captain was just about to tell everyone through his headset radio to stop and take a small break when suddenly, voices from the river area stopped him and Tracks who had also heard the voices dead where they stood.

The captain quietly told everyone through his headset to get low and stay quiet, that they had company. The soldiers all hit their bellies, each one with their rifles at the ready. The captain tapped Tracks on the shoulder and signaled for Tracks to follow him. They each pulled out their pistols, and off crawled the captain with Tracks right behind him. The trail they had been following was only about thirty yards from the river's edge. So the captain and Tracks had no problem crawling close enough to see whose voice they had heard.

Two canoes each full of Manduno warriors, every one of them armed with long spears and bow and arrows, paddled past them. The captain and Tracks were close enough to see the white of the warrior's eyes, and each of their faces had been painted with brilliant war paint. The warriors were intently looking at the riverbanks, looking for any movement and probably even looking for them. Luckily, the thick brush and reeds the captain and Tracks were looking at the warriors through hid them from the canoes' wandering eyes.

One of the warriors, most likely the leader, was standing up yelling out commands. At least that is how the captain and Tracks took it since they couldn't understand exactly what he had said. The captain and Tracks laid low and remained perfectly still and quiet until the canoes were completely out of sight. Just as they were about to crawl back to the other men, the unexpected happened.

A green mamba snake, a very long and skinny green snake and one of the Congo's most deadly and highly toxic snakes, crawled over the captain's shoulder and stopped, its long forked tongue flickering in and out.

Luckily, Tracks had seen it. "Do not move, Cap. Do not even blink," Tracks whispered into his headset radio and told the captain. The captain froze as he heard the terror in Tracks's voice. Tracks held his breath and waited for just the right moment. He slowly gripped the handle of his razor-sharp machete. As soon as the unsuspecting snake crawled a bit farther and placed its green little head back onto the jungle floor, Tracks, with a lightning speed flip of his machete, removed the head of the deadly green mamba.

The captain who had not seen the snake until Tracks had removed its head could now feel the nine-foot headless body of the serpent coiling and thrashing across his back. The captain quickly turned over and threw the lifeless but mobile body of the snake into the brush beside them. Tracks used his machete to dig a little hole in the soft wet ground where they laid. He then scraped the wide part of the blade across the ground, sweeping the deadly little green snake head into the hole. As he did this, the mouth of the snake's head closed around the edge of the blade. Tracks actually had to shake the machete a few times to dislodge the head from the blade.

Tracks looked over at the captain. "That's why you always remove and bury the heads. Dumb things can bite you even after you kill them. Rattlesnakes back home are the worst. Several hours after you kill one of them, their nerves make them still capable of thrashing and striking out blindly and sinking their poisonous fangs deep inside you. The only dead snake in my book is a headless one," Tracks told the captain.

"Thank you, sir. You saved my life," were the first words out of the captain's mouth.

"That was nothing, Cap. Let's just consider us square. You saved my life this morning," Tracks happily told the captain in his normal heavy southern draw. The captain reached over and shook Tracks's hand and patted him on the shoulder.

"Well, thanks anyhow, sir, the captain said again.

Tracks nodded his head in acknowledgement of the captain's deep-felt thanks, and then he started crawling back to the other men with the captain right behind him. When they reached the others, the captain explained to everyone what they had seen and how Tracks had saved his life. He then explained to everyone that in his best estimate that they were still two or three hours away from the rendezvous point. He also told everyone he was very worried about running into more Manduno warriors the closer they got to their village. The captain said he could tell that the warriors they had seen appeared to be looking for someone or something.

The captain said all they could do was continue as they have been and pray they make it to the others without any trouble. The captain asked Tracks to stay at the lead, and as everyone slowly stood up to head out, they each paused and cautiously looked around before once again off they went through the jungle, traveling as quietly and as fast as they could.

Back with Chandler and Tab's team, in the cave just above the river and the Manduno village, everyone was still sound asleep. Just seconds before Chandler and Otto's watch alarms could go off, the volcano decided to wake everybody up.

The Wait

The volcano started rumbling and shaking just enough to rain a little bit of dust and gravel-size debris down on everyone. But it certainly was enough to get everyone on their feet. As soon as Chandler's and Otto's feet hit the ground and they stood up, their watch alarms simultaneously began going off.

Chandler looked Otto square in the eyes and poked Otto's shoulder with his finger. "Get up," Chandler said jokingly.

"Good morning, sir," Otto said, ignoring the unusual attempt at humor from Chandler. As each member of the team slowly started fully waking up, everyone started putting away all their nonessential gear like the night vision goggles. Everyone was also getting out the lightweight jackets that just happened to be part of the normal gear in their backpacks.

It felt almost cold out this morning—way cooler than when they arrived only several hours before. In all of Tab's years living in this rainforest, this certainly was the coldest she had ever felt it. Chandler and Otto slowly approached the cave entrance and peered out. The cave's entrance not only overlooked the river perfectly but also a good portion of the Manduno village as well.

Otto started trying to reach the captain through the CB radio and then on his headset radio, but the only reply he got on both was static.

"Maybe they are still just out of range. They still have a couple of hours to get here," Chandler said, holding up his arm to look at his watch. "Lets not start to worry until we need to. They'll probably all show up here in a little while," he told Otto.

After Anvil and Bull got their backpacks in order and put away everything they didn't need, they walked over to Roy and Tab to say good morning. Shadow, not wanting to be left out, pushed his way in between everybody. Bull immediately started loving on the enormous beast.

Bull then stepped back and patted his big chest, wanting Shadow to stand up against him on his back legs. Now Bull is a very big broad man, weighing 325 pounds and all muscle. He stands six foot eight inches tall without his boots or his army helmet on. But when Shadow stood up against Bull, Shadow towered a good two foot over Bull's helmet, and Bull was wearing his boots. It took all Bull could muster to even hold him upright.

This black panther was no ordinary black panther. He was a goliath, a king among his kind.

Anvil looked at Roy and shook his head. "I'm glad he's on our side. I've never seen anything make Bull look small," Anvil told Roy.

"That's for sure, Anvil. Shadow is one huge cat. Tab could practically ride him like a horse," Roy commented back.

Bull laughed. "Wouldn't that be an awesome sight to see, Tab riding around on Shadow's back?" Bull said.

After Bull played with Shadow for a little while, everyone enjoyed some small talk. Afterward, Anvil and Bull walked back over and stood by Chandler and Otto who was still looking out the caves entrance. Otto's other three Special Forces soldiers were stationed at the two tunnel entranceways inside the cave, keeping their flank protected. Those three were all business and mostly kept to themselves.

Otto was just the opposite; he was outgoing, and he liked to be up front and in the thick of things. Chandler admired Otto for those characteristics. Chandler liked working with confident and intelligent people who could hold their own. Chandler could tell if a fight broke out that Otto was the kind of man you could depend on.

Roy, Tab, and Shadow sat down against the cave wall, and Shadow put his big head in Tab's lap. The big cat yawned and, in doing so, opened his mouth so wide Tab could have fit her entire head inside it.

Wow, I'd hate to be bit by that huge mouth, Roy thought to himself. Shadow had, at a minimum, seven-inch canines. Tab rubbed Shadow's head and nose until her furry friend was fast asleep. Staying up all night guarding everyone had finally caught up with Shadow, and he was out cold. He removed his enormous and heavy head off Tab's lap and curled up like a big house cat on a couch. Tab was thankful he moved on his own because he was getting heavy.

Anvil and Bull came back over to Roy and Tab and asked if they minded some more company. Seemed everyone was getting anxious and bored just waiting around. Tab quickly told them both to sit down. Bull asked Tab how she was holding up. Tab replied she was doing great but that she was a little worried about Tracks and the others. Anvil said he was worried too and he wished they'd just come on and get here. Bull was worried too, but seeing the down looks on Tab's and Anvil's face, he decided not to comment on their not being here and to change the subject.

"Hey, Tab, you got any more good prophecies about the Manduno tribe you could tell us about? I loved that last one you told us," Bull asked Tab.

"Well, yeah Bull, I know a bunch. Let's see if I can think of a really good one you might like. Oh yeah, how about my favorite one first told by the Manduno water witch centuries ago? It is the oldest prophecy the Manduno people have," Tab told Bull.

CHAPTER 31

The Water Witch

"Yes, ma'am, that sounds like a good one. Tell that one please," Bull said with an almost-childlike excitement.

"The best part of this prophecy is the sidenote that only the Manduno people know about," Tab told them.

"What's the sidenote?" her father Roy, asked her.

"It's that every single other prophecy that this witch doctor woman has ever told has came true—with the exception of this one I am about to tell you," Tab answered her father.

"Wow, how many did the water witch predict correctly?" Anvil then asked.

"Thirty-nine right on the money down to the smallest details. From disasters, afflictions, earthquakes, and even the last two times this old volcano had erupted. She was called Mayl Ndoki, which translates to the water witch. She was called this because she always saw her visions in the reflections of still water. She is, by far, the most famous of any of the Manduno witch doctors, man or woman. And who is to say this prophecy I am about to tell you just hasn't happened yet?" Tab told everyone.

The more Tab spoke, the more everyone's curiosity got the better of them. And before long, everyone in the cave had gathered around close enough to hear Tab tell her favorite Manduno water witch prophecy.

"Let me start by saying that the Manduno people have no written language. This story as well as all the countless other stories only still exist today because they have all been constantly repeated and retold as they have been done so for centuries," Tab told everyone before she began telling the actual story. "I am not sure exactly when this prophecy was first told, but it is at least two thousand years old."

Tab knew this to be a true statement because the first time she lived with the Manduno tribe was over nineteen hundred years ago. And it was an old prophecy back then when she first heard it.

"It is said that the water witch was alone high on top of this very volcano. She was there trying to gather special berries she knew only grew near the top. It is said she needed the berries to make the queen of the Manduno people a fertility potion as the queen was nearing her eighteenth birthday and had yet to bear the king a child.

"On her decent back down the volcano after gathering her much-needed berries, she came across several eagle feathers that had fell down from an eagle's nest high up on a towering ledge. This was a lucky find for her as eagles were and still are worshipped as protectors of the Manduno people. And eagle feathers are thought to carry powerful and mystical powers inside them.

"They are treasured as good luck charms by members of any tribe here in the Congo who happens to find them. But to a witch doctor, man or woman, to find several at one time would be the equivalent to you or me as hitting a lottery. They were and still are used in everything, from magic potions, medicines, and even in the making of charms to ward off evil spirits, bad luck, or unexplained afflictions.

"The water witch was excited as she crawled around on the wet ground, picking up the feathers. As she leaned over a small puddle of water to reach for the last of the feathers she had found, the water witch thought she saw another feather in the bottom of the puddle. As she gazed deep into the still water, looking hard for the prized eagle feather she thought she had seen, she was suddenly whisked away centuries into her people's future.

"She first saw thick hazy smoke blowing in the wind low to the ground. As the smoke slowly began to clear, she could see the top of the volcano, Mantoro, the volcano god, was angry and was unleashing his wrath. Lava flowed down from the volcano towards the river, igniting the jungle ferociously all along its path. The water witch could tell she was standing in her village because of the volcano towering above her. But it was different. This village was huge, and she immediately knew this was a glimpse of her people's future.

"Suddenly, she was whisked away again. This time, she was standing in a tribal counsel meeting. She heard the counsel arguing, a white man had been captured on the Manduno's southernmost boarder. The captured man seemed extremely ill and incoherent. But with Mantoro being so angry, the warriors thought that a white man so seldom seen in their territory might just be the perfect sacrifice to appease their volcano god's anger. But now it seemed that whatever had made the white man sick was now quickly spreading and affecting the entire village.

"The argument it seemed, was over a person of royalty, maybe a king that had been captured a few days previous. Manduno law clearly stated that all captured royalty be treated as such for at least six days before being beheaded. But it seemed to the water witch that most of the counsel wanted to sacrifice the king to Mantoro that evening instead of waiting and beheading him according to Manduno law. They argued that Mantoro's anger may have something to do with the sickness. And they thought that sacrificing a king to Mantoro would surely regain his favor. To the water witch, it looked like the two counsel members who wanted to follow the law were losing the fight.

"Right then, she was whisked away again. This time, it was dark outside. She was standing high atop the same sacrificial arena she had watched be built back in her time. Torches lit the area. Not one but several white men stood with their hands tied behind their backs. Each man unwillingly waited for their turn to be sacrificed.

"They were to be sacrificed to Mantoro, the volcano god, to appease his anger. The king was among this group of white men. Just as the Manduno executioner raised his axe high above his head to behead the first of the white men, the one who had brought the deadly affliction into their village, a mighty roar of a night god called out to the Manduno people.

"The water witch could not believe what she was seeing: there on a small trail sat an eagle lady atop the back of the god. The winged lady spoke so the Manduno people could understand her. The winged one said she was here to save the Manduno people. Everybody but the savage white men went to their knees, heads bowed. Never had such a sight been seen.

"Once again, the water witch was whisked away, and as quickly as it had all started, the vision ended. The water witch was back on her hands and knees, still starring down into the puddle of water where it had all began. She knew that her people's continued survival would someday be tested. And that only by allowing this eagle lady of a distant tomorrow to help them would her people have any hope of surviving this future affliction. She made her people learn and retell this prophecy so that when the day of the prophecy came to be fulfilled, her people would be ready.

"Those eagle feathers she found that day are still among the current witch doctor's treasures, having been passed down through out the centuries. The water witch, though never having heard their names, made a drawing of the white man's name and of the winged ladies name as both were drawn on each of the garments each had been wearing—"

"Tab, you know so many languages, and I bet you've no doubt seen these drawings. What did the names say?" Chandler interrupted and asked.

"Yes, I have seen the drawings of the names made by the water witch, but I couldn't make anything out of what she wrote. She must have seen the names wrong. They do not spell anything or anyone's name in any written language," Tab explained.

Otto got everyone thinking when he said, "We're white men, and the volcano god, Mantoro, is definitely teed off right now. I wonder if it's us she was talking about," he implied. Everyone laughed at Otto's suggestion, but deep down, it made them all start to think.

Chandler, in turn, added, "It makes no sense for the water witch to get the names wrong if she's as good as you said she was Tab. There has to be an angle. Something we just aren't seeing," Chandler questioned.

"It's a two-thousand-year-old prophecy. I wouldn't get too tore up about it. There doesn't seem to be any sickness here—no captured white men. And I certainly do not think we will see any eagle ladies come riding up on any god's back. Come on, guys. Let's keep it real," Roy commented.

Chandler tried to clarify what he had meant earlier. "I'm just saying, Roy, how could the water witch have had thirty-nine perfect predictions then mess up two simple names? I'm not saying we're the prophecy—I was just commenting on it," Chandler said.

Otto drifted back over to the cave entrance and peered down. "Hey, everyone, you're not going to believe this, but come check this out," Otto said.

CHAPTER 32

A Prophecy Unfolds

Down below, a huge crowd of Manduno villagers had gathered to meet a group of warriors coming back from a hunt. From their viewpoint high above the village, they could see two warriors carrying what appeared to be a body tied and dangling down from a large stick that they carried over their shoulders. The man, a white man, appeared dead. Chandler quickly grabbed a pair of binoculars, fearing the man was one of his. Upon closer inspection, he could see that the man was not one of his but just a random individual probably in the wrong place at the wrong time. He did see the man struggling, so he knew the man was alive, at least for now.

"Who is it? Is it?" asked Otto, who was interrupted by Chandler.

"He's not one of ours. I don't know who the poor guy is. He is alive though," Chandler told everyone.

Anvil had a worried thought. "Did he look sick?" Anvil asked. The second the words came out of his mouth, everyone turned and looked at each other. Now everyone was curious of the man's condition. Chandler started to blow off Anvil's question, but something made him grab his binoculars and look again.

From the distance, they were from the crowd below, and even with his really good pair of binoculars, Chandler just couldn't tell much about the man's condition.

"I just can't tell, Anvil. We're too far away. The guy does look very angry though." Chandler almost said, "Fit to be tied." This wasn't the time for humor, and Chandler knew it. He knew he must be getting a little nervous though because he always had the bad habit of trying to bring unwanted humor into any difficult situations he would find himself in.

Otto looked at Chandler. "I'm really getting worried about the captain and the others now. That prophecy is really freaking me out, sir," said Otto.

"If our guys show up on sticks, I'll freak out with you. Until then, let's not make more out of this than there is," said Chandler as he tried to reassure Otto and everyone else.

Since Anvil asked if the man was sick, Tab's mind had been racing. This seemed like way more than just a coincidence to her. Tab sat back against the cave wall and started going over every aspect of the prophecy. It had always seemed so surreal every time she had ever previously heard it. An eagle lady riding on a god's back—that's the part that always made the prophecy seem so unreal to her. It just sounded like a fantasy story, not something in the realm of rational thinking. But as she sat and petted Shadow, it suddenly seemed so much more possible.

Black panthers have always been considered living night gods by the Manduno people. And the fact that if she herself had been seen by the water witch two thousand years ago in this prophecy in her true angelic form, then she could have been easily mistaken as an eagle lady. And then there was the joke earlier made by her father and Bull about her riding Shadow. Also now, a white man just came in captured, and our president just got captured two days ago. Tab knew they would have considered him either royalty or a king.

Oh no, she thought, *the captured white man was supposed to have had an affliction. He was captured in the Manduno's most southern border, and that's almost Northern Angola. Northern Angola is where the blue boil outbreak is taking place. Oh no,* she thought again the temperature is so cool outside. *This is bad, so bad.*

Tab quickly stood up and went over to her father. She grabbed him by his hand and led him into the closest cave out of sight and, in almost a panicked whisper, said to him, "Dad, you've got to get out of here right now. Please, Dad, take off and go back to Mom." Her eyes welled up with tears as she spoke to him.

Her dad grabbed both of her arms. "Tab, what's wrong with Christina?" he asked her.

"Nothing is wrong with mom, Dad. It's not her—it's all of us here. We're all going to die, Dad. Mom needs you, Dad, and I can't bear the thought of her being alone. Please go back to her before it's too late," Tab explained.

Tab's father, Roy pulled his daughter into his arms and hugged her tightly. "We're okay, Tab. What makes you think we're all going to die?" her father asked her.

"It's the prophecy, Dad. We are the prophecy. I am the prophecy," Tab said as she wiped the tears from her eyes.

"Tab, is this what this is all about? Honey, it's just an old story, and that's all," her father said, trying to calm her down.

"No Dad, it's real, and it's here. The man that they captured has the blue boil disease. And feel how cold it is outside, Dad? You know what that means? It means were all going to die. I'm going to fail trying to save the President because he's going to die with us," Tab explained to her father.

"How do you know the man has the blue boil affliction, Tab? Chandler couldn't tell, so what makes you think he has it?" her father questioned her.

"Because I know—because I am the prophecy," Tab told him.

Roy just couldn't believe what he was hearing, "Then who's the eagle lady that is supposed to come riding in on a God. I thought she was the prophecy," her father asked her.

"The eagle lady is the prophecy Dad, but what I am trying to tell you is I am the eagle lady," Tab said, trying to make her father understand.

"Not trying to burst your bubble here, baby girl, but in no way do you look like an eagle lady to me. I don't see any wings on you, and who is this night god you're supposed to come riding in on?" asked her father, trying to convince himself as much as his daughter that she must be wrong.

"Shadow, Dad. Remember the totem pole? Back panthers are worshipped by the Manduno people as night gods. And about the wings." Tab paused for a long moment and then just decided to come totally clean and tell him everything.

CHAPTER 33

The Confession

"I normally have wings, Dad," Tab confessed. Roy stepped back and tried to make sense out of what Tab had just told him.

"Wings, what are you talking about? How do you normally have wings? You're losing me on this one, baby girl. Help me catch up, and tell me what you talking about," her father asked her.

"I'm an angel Dad, a real life angel normally with wings who normally lives in heaven with God, My heavenly Father. And oh, how I miss him Dad. God is so amazing, and he loves me so much, and he's so good to me and to all of us up in heaven. And the first task he gives me, I fail him," Tab said as she started breaking down at the thought of failing her Heavenly Father God.

Her father Roy, felt her sorrow and pulled her back into his arms and once again hugged her tightly trying to calm her down. "You're serious, aren't you Tab? You're really telling me the truth," he said as he continued holding her tightly.

Tab nodded her head as she continued to sob in her father's arms. Her father started trying to think of ways to cheer up his baby girl; he hated seeing her so tore up.

"Hey, I love you too baby girl, and you haven't failed anything yet. You remember all those late nights me and you stayed up doing your so-called impossible school projects? And if I remember correctly, we got As on almost every one of them, didn't we?" her father, Roy, asked her.

Tab nodded her head again, already feeling better from her father's pep talk.

"Maybe this is why we're together. Maybe God knows what a good team we make. So let's figure this out together. Okay, baby girl? I will help you. I love helping you," her father told her.

Tab looked up and smiled at her father as she dried her eyes. "You're right as usual, Dad. Let's do this," Tab said, finally smiling.

"Okay then, but for starters, I would love to see your wings. Can you show me?" her father Roy asked.

"No, Dad, I wish I could, but I am just a human right now. I've got none of my angelic powers except for my perfect memory," Tab explained to her father.

"The water witch must have seen wings if she thought you were some type of an eagle lady," her father commented.

"I know I don't get it. I don't understand how she could have seen my wings with me as just a human," Tab said, frustrated.

"Maybe you're just a human right now, but maybe by tonight, you won't be. That's the only answer there can be, baby girl. Somehow, by tonight, you find a way to get your wings," her father confidently told her.

Suddenly, Shadow came around the corner of the tunnel they were talking in and stood by Tab. Seeing Shadow standing by his daughter gave Roy a thought and an angle to attack their unusual situation. "You say you're just a human, but how many humans can talk to animals? How many humans can predict earthquakes or say they know God on a personal basis? How many humans know every language ever spoken since time began?" her father asked her.

Tab looked deep into her father's eyes. "What are you saying, Dad?" Tab asked.

"I'm saying that if your heavenly powers are limited by your being human, then there are earthly rules that can give you heavenly powers," her father said, almost excited for Tab to ask him what he meant.

"What do you mean?" asked Tab.

"Faith, baby girl faith," her father said, smiling. "The Bible says 'faith the size of a mustard seed can move a mountain.' 'Just humans' have to dig deep sometimes to believe in a deity they have never seen before or only read about in a Bible several thousand years old. But an angel, a counselor to all of God's creations who has walked the streets of heaven, how much faith would they have? An eternal being who lives in heaven and who knows God personally, how much faith would they have?

"An actual angel's faith would come from knowing, not believing. Why, Tab, I'd say that an angel's faith would be the size of a mountain, if not even bigger, not the size of a tiny mustard seed. I wonder what obstacles could faith the size of a mountain move," her father said, now on a roll with his pep talk.

"Remember the prophecy said that none of the Manduno people would survive if not for the eagle lady? So you do find a cure or some way to help beat this blue boil disease. And even though the water witch never said it, I have faith you will somehow save the rest of us too. Maybe your earthly doubts are all that is limiting your heavenly abilities. Lose your doubts, baby girl, and embrace your enormous faith you've always had in God, and do what you have always done at least since I've known you," her father told her.

"What's that, dad?" asked Tab.

"Succeed," he said. "Let's get back before everybody starts missing us," Roy said as he gave her one more big hug.

"I'll try my best to get us another A, Dad. Thank you so much. You have always been there for me, and I love you so much," Tab told her father.

"I love you too, baby girl, and I know you will do your best. That's all anyone can ask of someone," her father told her.

Shadow, who was still standing beside Tab, snuggled his huge head up against her shoulder and looked at her. Standing on all fours, Shadow still stood head high to Tab.

Tab looked back at Shadow. "I know you'll be there for me too, and I love you too," she told her big furry friend.

The trio walked back into the main cave where everyone else still was.

"A little family meeting, I see. Is everything all right?" Chandler asked.

"More like a prayer meeting," Roy replied.

Chandler nodded his head and turned back toward the cave entrance. Roy, Tab, and Shadow walked back over to where Anvil and Bull was sitting. Now it was Tab that asked them if they minded a little company.

"Please sit down, you guys," Bull said. After everyone was sat down and was as comfortable as possible.

Anvil looked over at Tab. "Going back to what Chandler had said earlier about it not making sense that the water witch would mess up two simple names. Well, I've been thinking. What if the names were spelled backwards?" Anvil asked Tab. Before Tab had a chance to answer Anvil, Chandler jumped in the conversation.

"What do you mean spelled backwards? Why would you think that?" asked Chandler who had been listening from the cave entrance.

"Because she's the water witch who saw all her visions in the reflection of still water and all reflections show things in reverse. So, logically, it would seem to me that anything she would have seen including the names would have had to appear backwards to her. If her vision was about to go down, it might be simple English just written backwards," Anvil told everyone listening.

Tab immediately grabbed a paper and pen and wrote down the water witch's markings. Tab then held up the paper and turned it over to look through the thin paper and clearly saw two names wrote out, Watson and Tab.

Tab's father saw her expression change as she held up the thin paper. He knew even without being told that somehow one of the names on it would be hers.

"Does it say something you can decipher?" Chandler asked. Tab, not knowing what to say, looked at her father for help.

"Just show them, Tab. You've got nothing to be ashamed of or, at this late stage of the game, to hide," her father told her.

Tab, still looking at her father, asked, "Everything?"

"Yeah, baby girl, just tell them," her father replied.

"Tell us what? This isn't the time to be holding out, you two," Chandler said sternly! Tab, in response, reached the small paper with the two names on it over to Chandler. Chandler took the paper from

Tab's hand and held it up toward the light coming from the cave entrance to see through the paper.

"What's it say?" asked Anvil.

"I bet one of the names says Tab," Bull said confidently.

"One says Watson, and the other says Tab," Chandler told everyone with a shocked look on his face. Everybody in the cave stared right at Tab.

"Tab, what's going on? And I want the truth—lives are at stake here," Chandler demanded of Tab.

Tab felt everyone's eyes on her, and after a long pause, she said, "I know I know. It seems I am the prophecy and all of you are a part of it also," Tab told everybody. Tab then went into great detail and told everyone everything from the blue boil disease to her angelic alter ego. She did leave out everyone else's heavenly alter ego as somehow she sensed God would not want that known. Surprising enough to Tab, with everything everyone had already seen from her, everybody took it better than she expected.

Bull just kept saying under his breath, "I knew it, I knew it." Chandler and everyone else just sat in silence and stared at Tab for a couple of moments, letting everything she had told them sink in and register.

Chandler broke the silence, "What's this mean for us? What do we need to do?" Chandler asked Tab.

CHAPTER 34

The Script

"The script has already been written, and unfortunately, like it or not, we all have a role to play in it," Tab answered Chandler.

"What do you mean by that? Just what is our role going to be?" Chandler asked, still unsure as to just what he and his team were supposed to do.

"Well, you may not like this answer, but here goes. The captain, Tracks, and their team will be standing up on the sacrificial arena tonight getting ready to be beheaded. Or everybody in this cave will be up there, with the exception of Shadow and me. Worst-case scenario could put both teams up there with your hands tied behind your backs. The water witch did say there were several white men and the king standing up on the arena. And with only nine of you men out of both teams that are Caucasian, that small number of men could easily have been viewed as just several men.

"Wow, so no matter what we do, it probably won't matter. Whether we run, hide or stay, and fight, we'll probably still end up there just like the water witch saw over two thousand years ago," Chandler said, aggravated.

"What we do from this point on will matter to God. Chandler, if this is something he wants us to do, then I am not running or hiding. If I die trying to do his will, then so be it. I couldn't think of a better death. You can count me in, Tab," Otto said, and no one in the cave doubted his sincerity.

Anvil and Bull both looked at Tab. "You know we're both in, Tab," Anvil said.

Bull held up his enormous bicep to proudly show off his tattoo to everyone. "We're guardians of God's angels," Bull said. The moment the words came out of his mouth, both Anvil and Bull had the very same thought and at the very same time. Had their tattoos been meant for Tab as well as the little orphans? It seemed an awful big coincidence if not. They both smiled at that thought and shook their heads in unison. Now no matter what the outcome, they knew they were in this thing until the end.

Chandler was in deep thought as to his feelings on this matter ever since Otto had spoken up. Chandler had always been a loner and the kind of man that hated to lose. So the thought of being captured and having his hands tied behind his back wasn't setting too good with him. And then there was the blue boil disease, and no way did he want any part of that stuff. Just the thought of that stuff made him want to bail and head back home.

But on the other hand, he knew he was almost fifty-eight years old, and he was smart enough to know he wasn't going to live forever. And with his not-so-perfect past, he knew this might be his only chance at some sort of redemption. After all, how often does someone get an opportunity to help God personally? The decision was an easy one for Chandler—he was in.

"You can count me in too, Tab. How can someone say no to God?" Chandler told Tab. One by one, everybody on the team told Tab to count them in. Everybody had said yes to Tab but one, her father.

Tab turned to her father, already knowing what his answer would be, and she could feel the torment and ache in his heart, fearing his answer would hurt her. He knew Tab wanted him to run back home to her mother, so there was no chance of her being hurt and left alone should things go wrong. But he was not only a man but he was a man of God. If God needed him here, then here he would stay.

Roy leaned down and kissed Tab on the cheek. "Sorry, baby girl, but count me in too, and even if you weren't my daughter, I couldn't leave knowing I had a chance to help God. Your mother would understand and back this decision ten out of ten times, and you know it, and I hope you'll try to understand too," her father told her.

"I do understand, Dad, and you're right about Mom. Now I have to get that A, don't I?" Tab said as she hugged her father tightly.

"Doubting you won't is the only thing that can stop you. Just remember you've got faith the size of a mountain," he told her.

"It's settled then. We're all in. Now the next question is how are you going to save all of us tonight, Tab?" Chandler asked her.

"I can't save you, Chandler, and I can't save anybody else tonight either," Tab told him. "You all need to understand something right now. This isn't about me—this is about the glory of God Almighty. You all may see me tonight up on that hillside riding Shadow, but if anybody gets saved tonight, it will be by the hand of God that it happens, not by mine. The one thing I can tell you all is I know my Heavenly Father God well enough to know that if I am the vessel he uses to save us tonight, then he will somehow show me the way and at a time of his choosing.

CHAPTER 35

Salvation

The fact that you all have agreed to risk everything and help God is awesome, but only God knows how tonight will turn out. So if any of you men aren't saved and haven't as of yet accepted his Son Jesus Christ as your Savior, then before this evening would be a really good time to do so. I could help any of you with that if you'd like me to. To put one's faith and trust in our Lord Jesus Christ and accept him as your Savior is one of the simplest and most rewarding things a man or woman can ever do," Tab told everyone.

"I was saved as a kid, but I'd like to get saved again, if that's allowed," Bull softly asked Tab.

"It's always okay to confess your love and commitment to our Lord Jesus Christ and to accept him as your Lord and Savior," Tab told Bull.

"I think we would all like to get saved or saved again, if you could help us do that," Chandler asked Tab as he had never before been saved.

"Does everyone here feel the same way?" Tab asked everyone around her.

Everybody told Tab they did, and they all gathered closer to her. Tab reached out both of her hands, and after everyone formed a circle, she asked everyone to close their eyes. With a happy heart, Tab began guiding everyone into eternal salvation and everlasting life. Salvation that can only be found by accepting Jesus Christ as your

Lord and Savior and accepting the gift of his sacrifice that day long ago when he was hung on a cross and died for everyone's sins.

After it was over, everyone still held hands for a few minutes longer, each just enjoying the new sensation of being reborn and of the new comradely of being brothers through Christ.

Bull broke the silence and raised his arms high above his head, causing everyone to do the same. "We are all soldiers of Christ and warriors of God. Now watch out, everybody," Bull said as his enthusiasm busted out from his big heart. "Amen, everybody," Bull continued.

"Amen," everyone told Bull back.

Tab, seeing Bull so happy being filled with the Holy Spirit, made her cry tears of joy. Tab felt this huge rush of joy come over her. She felt so good helping these men get saved and accept Jesus Christ as their Savior. If this was to be her job for all of eternity, then she wanted to work double shifts.

As the men went back about their business, Tab sat down beside Shadow. She was still on cloud nine, and she just wanted to sit down, pet her big furry friend, and silently talk to God for a little while. Tab had a lot of questions about tonight, way more questions than she had answers for. Tab truly had faith that her Heavenly Father God would show her the way and that no matter how this all turned out tonight that he would know that she had done her best to make him proud.

CHAPTER 36

A Trap Is Set

Back over to the captain, Tracks, and their team as they trekked through the jungle. Each now followed tightly to the man in front of them, trying to move as one unit and not spread out like before. Unknown to the men, the trail they were on just happened to be one of the Manduno's main thoroughfares and was heavily patrolled.

Tracks and his team had made it about an hour from their rendezvous point when their luck finally ran out. A lone Manduno scout running lead to a very large group of Manduno warriors had climbed a large tree to get a better bird's eye view of the trail and area ahead. It only took the scout a few moments to catch a glimpse of Tracks and his team ducking and dodging as they headed his way.

The scout raised both of his hands up to his mouth, right under a large toothpick of a bone that had been pierced right through the nose of the Manduno scout. He started imitating a jungle snipe's call perfectly, a common Congo parrot-like bird. Back down the trail, the first warrior in line, their leader, heard the scout and threw up his hand and stopped his very large group of warriors in their tracks. As soon as his hand went up, there was complete silence, not even a single sound was made by any of his warriors. They all just stood there, almost motionless, only turning their heads slightly from side to side, trying to decipher the scout's hidden messages.

Suddenly and a few hand gestures later, he and all his warriors slowly stepped off the trail and disappeared into the jungle. Several warriors even climbed up into the canopy completely hidden from view just feet from where the approaching and unsuspecting victims' heads would be. The trap was set, and it was set tight.

Tracks and his team had been moving along well and without incident. They knew they were getting really close to meeting back up with Chandler and the rest of their friends. This thought had pepped up their spirits and gave them all a much-needed second wind. Tracks was still on the lead, and although he was no longer setting a blistering pace, he had his team moving pretty well.

Suddenly and out of nowhere, a lone Manduno warrior stepped out onto the trail about a hundred feet in front of Tracks and the team. The lanky man appeared unarmed and just stood there and stared at them, his hands at his sides.

Tracks stopped as soon as the tribal warrior stepped out onto the trail. Tracks and the captain looked at each other, perplexed by the man's reaction or, to say the least, lack of reaction. Tracks started to pull his revolver, but as he reached for it, the Captain covered his hand, not allowing Tracks to remove the pistol from its holster.

"Sir, he's not carrying a spear, so I don't think a gun is necessary. Let's not frighten him away. Let's just get close enough to grab him," the captain said, almost whispering.

"Then what do we do with him? Take him with us?" Tracks asked back in a whisper.

"I don't know, Maybe just tie him up real good and gag him and leave him off the trail a good ways. Maybe in a day or so, some of his people will find him. I hate to just kill him, sir," the captain explained to Tracks.

As Tracks nodded his head in agreement to the captain's plan, he and his team slowly edged their way toward the man getting ever so closer. The man appeared almost frozen as he held his ground and continued to stare straight at them. When Tracks and his team got within twenty feet of the man, the man whom up to that moment had not so much moved even a finger now clearly and purposely smiled at all of them.

Everyone instantly knew the meaning of that smile. And before any of them could even react, a multitude of very long and sharpened spearheads had emerged from every direction and was only inches from their faces.

"Stand down," the Captain told his men, fearing one or all would go for a weapon. As the captain told his men that, a finely honed, sharpened spearhead closed the gap and indented the skin on his neck, causing a very small bright red trickle of blood to flow down from the point of the spearhead. The captain closed his eyes and gritted his teeth, fearing the worst.

Soon, the spearhead backed off a few inches, and he realized that was just their way of telling him to shut his mouth or else. It only took a few minutes, and the Manduno warriors had the entire team gagged and bound. Each man had their hands tied behind their backs with small but extremely strong rope-like vines. And the gags that was used was some sort of wet bulbous type of root that was forced into each of their mouths and tied around their heads to keep them lodged in place.

The gags not only tasted like medicine, but almost instantly, each man started getting lightheaded. And even though they knew they were being drugged, they could do little to stop it. Soon, all six men were in a zombie-like state. Their eyes were rolled so far back in their heads that only the whites could be seen, giving them all the classic zombie appearance.

The Manduno liked administering this root to their captives because not only did it almost instantly remove any fight left in the prisoners, it stupefied them while still allowing them to function. They could walk and be led around like a pet spider monkey on a vine. Soon, the Manduno warriors had their captives subdued and were leading them back to their village. Happy and excited about their catch, the leader of the Manduno warriors sent the scout that had spotted the men back to their village to tell the tribal leaders and everyone the news.

CHAPTER 37

An Angel at Work

An hour later, back at the cave with Chandler and Tab's team, it was now 1300 hours and still no sign of the other team.

"What do we do now?" Otto asked Chandler.

"I say we follow the original plan. If we're going to get captured, then I say we may as well get captured at least trying to save the president," Chandler replied.

"I am up for anything that will get us out of this cave. I am so sick of just sitting and waiting," Otto told Chandler. Chandler nodded his head at Otto, and just as he was about to tell everybody to get set to move out, a loud commotion from the village below stopped him. Roy, who had just walked over to the caves entrance, excitedly spoke out.

"Chandler, you better come take a look, something's going on down in the village," Roy said. Chandler stepped over near Roy and looked down at the village with his binoculars. Otto came over and did the same thing. Through their binoculars, they could see villagers of all ages hurrying and scurrying about.

Suddenly, chanting and singing broke out from the crowd below followed almost immediately by tribal drums.

"Something's happening down there, but what?" Chandler asked.

"Yeah, but—hey, wait a minute—look towards the last hut near the river's edge," Otto told Chandler. Chandler panned back and forth, looking through the binoculars until he saw what Otto had asked him to look at. A large crowd of villagers was following a small Manduno man with a large bone pierced right through his nose. He appeared to be excitedly telling the crowd something as he walked with them, and whatever it was seemed to ignite the crowd's excitement. Tab walked up to the men at the caves entrance and looked out at the villagers down below.

"I wish I knew what he was telling them," Chandler said out loud.

"They've captured Tracks, the captain, and all of the other men to," Tab sadly told him.

"How do you know for sure what the little guy down there is telling them?" Anvil asked Tab.

"Yeah, how?" Otto asked.

"Actually, I do not know what that man down there is saying, but I do know what the drums are telling everyone. They're saying a large group of warriors caught six men in the jungle," Tab answered. Tab turned her head slightly to hear the drums over the chanting and singing to finish deciphering the message. "They also say the men are all alive and being led here as we speak," Tab told everyone.

Chandler started to say something, but Tab held up her hand and stopped him as she continued to concentrate hard, trying to follow the drums' messages. After a few minutes, Tab opened her eyes and pulled her attention away from the sounds of the drums.

"The drums are telling everyone to come to the sacrificial arena this evening. That tonight, all the captured men will be sacrificed to Mantoro, the volcano god," Tab regrettably told everyone.

"They got Tracks," Bull asked, not wanting to believe it.

"They might have him, Bull, but we'll get him back. You can bank on that and everybody else too," Anvil confidently told Bull.

"I promise you we will because old Bull ain't leaving this jungle until we do," replied Bull back just as confidently.

Everybody stood near the cave's entrance and avidly watched the village below. As much as everyone hated to see their friends and comrades captured and bound, they all needed to at least see that they were alive. Tab could feel the high level of anxiety coming from everyone around her.

Suddenly, and to her surprise, she could somehow now read each man's individual concerns: *Chandler was worried about everyone's welfare and that maybe he should have handled this whole mission differently. He was thinking he should have brought the whole army, not just the dozen or so of us. Otto was so nervous about seeing his comrades being brought in tied up like animals. His main concern was that his friends were not being mistreated.*

My father, Roy—God, love him—was mostly just worried about me, and he wished he had stood up to Chandler and just demanded that we had not went with him on this mission. Dad was also worried and thinking about Mom. He knew she would soon start to worry about the two of us if she didn't hear from him soon. He wished he had a way to call her.

Anvil and Bull was both taking the capture of Tracks pretty hard. The three of them had been like brothers for years now. Especially big softhearted Bull, he did not like the thought of anyone mistreating his friend. As Tab looked over at Bull, she saw him close his eyes and watched his face as the tension instantly melted away from it. Suddenly, as if he was talking to her, she could hear Bull's thoughts as he began praying to God.

It was the sweetest prayer ever, Tab thought as she heard Bull offer to trade his life for the life of his friend Tracks. Bull asked God to keep Tracks safe and not let anyone mistreat or hurt him. He prayed Tracks wasn't in any pain. Bull then told God he was sorry for not mentioning the other men, and he asked God to please protect them to. Before Bull said amen, Tab heard him ask God one more thing. Bull asked God to please help and watch over Tab tonight.

Wow, with all that was going on, Bull, was worried about me. Bull has such a big heart, Tab thought. Otto's three other men were not concerned about themselves at all either but about their captured comrades and of their families back home. Tab was overcome with all the thoughts everyone was unknowingly sharing with her, and she wished she could help each of them. She knew she had to find a way to ease everyone's concerns, to say something or do something, anything that would work.

Just as that thought entered Tab's mind, Otto, who was still scanning the village below with his binoculars broke her train of thought, "Hey, here they come, I think," Otto said excitedly.

Down below, a large group of warriors could be seen arriving into the village. It appeared that everyone in the village had lined up to welcome them home and to see their prisoners. Sure enough, right in the middle of the warriors was Tracks, the captain, and his other four Special Forces soldiers being marched right down into the middle of the village.

The village drums seemed to go into high gear along with the chanting and the singing as the warriors led their captives through the village to show them off like cattle at a sale.

"What's going on with our men? Something doesn't look right," Chandler said, looking through his binoculars.

"Yeah, they're walking funny, and their eyes look weird too," Otto added.

"It's the nee nee root making them act that way," Tab told everybody. "It's a round, gooey root the warriors make gags out of. When placed in a victim's mouth, the drug in the nee nee root basically turns them into mindless slaves. The good news is there is never any need to harm the captives because they are always so compliant. So I'm sure our guys will be okay until we can help set them free. The drug is harmless and will eventually just wear off," Tab told everyone, trying to ease their fears.

Then without thinking, Tab turned to Bull. "The drug is also a powerful pain reliever so Tracks and the others are diffidently not in any pain, Bull," Tab said to Bull.

"Thank you, Tab. That sure is good news to hear I've been so worried about Tracks. I was just talking to God a few minutes ago praying my buddy was not in any…" Suddenly, big Bull paused and looked over at Tab as he remembered he had silently prayed to God. "Pain," Bull softly said as he finished his statement, but as he said it, the look of bewilderment on his face enlightened Tab to her slip up.

Tab could tell Bull assumed what she had actually done, but she could also tell that he wasn't angry about it. After all, Tab thought to herself, she didn't mean to ease drop on anyone; it just happened. Tab continued feeling a little guilty for having made Bull feel uncomfortable. But to her defense, one of the many amazing things angels can do is hear the thoughts of anyone or anything in emotional distress. And as crazy as this may sound, but in the eons she has lived since her heavenly creation as an angel, this had been the first time she had ever had the ability to hear the thoughts of others.

After all, almost all her time alive had been spent in training down here on earth. And only angels who had graduated and finished their training ever gained the abilities to actually perform angelic duties for God, their Heavenly Father. This thought got Tab thinking: Did this mean she was done or at least almost done with her training? Could this be the last life she would ever live as an earthly human?

The thought of being done with her training and graduating was an instant emotional roller coaster for her. Tab loved coming to earth for training and experiencing the drama of all the different lives she had ever lived. She had been coming to earth for so long now it truly saddened her to think it might all be over, that she would never be reborn back into the world she had grown to love so much.

But on the flip side of this was the almost unimaginable joy and bliss of finally being able to fulfill her destiny and join the ranks of working-class angels. To spend one's life in the service of the Heavenly Father is the aspiration of every angel as that's why they exist in the first place. Either way, Tab knew it was in the hands of God. Only God alone knew when an angel was ready to perform to his standards and become a working-class angel.

Deep down, Tab had become excited about the prospect of graduating and joining her brother and sister angels that had already done so and had since taken up the family business of helping their Heavenly Father, God. Tab was lost in the thought of all the possibilities.

Chandler looked around the room, and he too could tell everyone was in deep thought and thinking about their friends down below. He knew it was time to do something and to get his team moving as there was no need to wait any longer.

CHAPTER 38

Time to Roll

"Okay, everybody, it looks like we are on our own now. It also looks like this prophecy thing were all mixed up in just got as real as it could get, which means I no longer feel we need to even try to go save the president as it is now obvious to me that he will be up there with our men tonight waiting to be executed. So to even attempt any kind of rescue of President Worsham would more than likely put us up there with him," Chandler told everyone.

"So what's our next move?" asked Otto.

"Our mission has, as of right now, changed, and our new number one priority is to simply keep Tab safe and to make sure the water witch sees her sitting up on top of Shadow tonight up on that hillside. The way I see it, the rest is out of our hands and in the hands of God and Tab," Chandler finished telling everyone.

"How are we going to get her all the way over to that hillside without being seen?" asked Otto.

"This cave can get us over to that hillside, and I know the way through the tunnels to get us there," Tab said excitedly.

"Perfect. Everybody, get ready to do a little exploring because we roll in ten," Chandler said as he started to put his binoculars back into their leather case. Chandler decided that everyone should use their night vision goggles for the trip through the tunnels. He was afraid if the team used flashlights, which everyone had, that their glow might accidentally be seen and cause them to be discovered.

Since Tab knew the way, she had the lead again, with Shadow and everyone else staying close to her. As usual Anvil and Bull brought up the rear to safeguard the team's flank. As the team got about two hundred yards into the cave, the volcano rumbled again and rained down debris from the ceiling of the cave just long enough to shake everybody up and scare poor Shadow to death.

"Is everyone okay?" Chandler asked, looking around at everybody.

"The caboose is okay," Bull replied.

"I'm good, but poor Shadow isn't a happy camper. I don't think he's a big fan of caves, especially ones falling in," Tab said from the front.

"Tell him I'm not either," Chandler told Tab.

Just like back in the sacred burial ground, Tab wasn't sure if it was the green tint of the night vision goggles or the fact that she knew she was walking around in complete darkness, but something in this cave had her on edge. Finally, up the tunnel a small ways, Tab could see the glow of a torch dancing on the cave wall. Tab whispered into her headset radio and told everyone to stay very quiet.

"What's going on?" Chandler asked.

"I can see light up ahead. We're getting close to where they might be holding the president," Tab answered Chandler.

Slowly, the team continued on toward the light until they reached a large handmade bamboo gate. The gate had obviously been built to block anyone from exiting or entering the tunnel system. Chandler eased his way up past Roy and Shadow to have a closer look. On the other side of the gate, they saw torches hung around the walls lighting up an extremely large cave room.

Two huge bamboo jail cells or cages best described what they saw inside of the cave. Unfortunately, both cells were empty, but Chandler pointed out to Tab that she had been right in thinking the president might be held here. The president's jacket was still hung up in one of the bamboo cells.

"I guess they probably already moved the president and all of the other men up to the arena. The Manduno have a huge holding cell up there also. It's only used when someone's getting sacrificed," Tab whispered to Chandler.

"Are there any tunnels that connect up to the arena area?" Chandler asked Tab under his breath.

"No, the closest is the one that comes out on the hillside near where Shadow and I are supposed to be tonight, but it isn't all that close to the arena area," Tab regrettably told Chandler.

"Well, let's get you over to where you need to be before something else goes wrong. Maybe we can at least do that," Chandler told Tab, sounding a little defeated with all that's gone wrong so far on this mission.

Tab reached out and put her small hand on Chandler's broad shoulder. "Chin up, everything's going to work out. I plan on getting an A tonight," Tab whispered to Chandler.

"God's grading you?" asked Chandler with a small chuckle.

"No, it's a father-daughter thing, just a little personal joke," Tab said, pointing to her father, Roy. Tab turned and quietly disappeared into the adjoining tunnel. Shadow fell back in behind her, followed by Roy. Then Chandler cut in front of Otto. He had decided to stay near the front where the action would no doubt be, if something happened or broke out. Plus, he knew Tab had said there was still another entrance into one more Manduno secret room, and he thought his place should be near the front.

The team turned a corner and came upon a section of tunnel that had collapsed almost completely shut. Most likely from the three or four earthquakes that's happened in the last few days. A small opening at the top of the huge pile of boulders and rocks that had blocked the way could be seen from below. Otto climbed up to see if the opening was big enough to squeeze through.

As he climbed the boulders and got closer to the top of the cave, he commented to everyone below, through his headset radio, how hot it was getting the higher he climbed. Otto also said he could see daylight coming in through some cracks in the ceiling above where the boulders had fell from.

When he finally reached the opening, he said it looked big enough to crawl through at least for everyone except maybe big Bull.

Otto said the heat was really intense coming out of the opening, but Chandler had everyone climb up anyway. Slowly but steadily and one by one, everyone made it up the boulders and through the small opening at the top. Luckily, it turned out the opening was big enough to allow Shadow and even big Bull to just squeeze through it. It looked so close that Anvil and Otto waited on the other side in case Shadow or Bull needed help and had to be pulled through.

As soon as Shadow and the three soldiers climbed down from the huge pile of boulders and their feet hit the ground, the volcano rumbled again. Like the previous earthquake, this one only lasted long enough to make a huge boulder that had hung above the small opening they had all just crawled through fall down, closing the opening completely shut.

"I guess we won't be coming back out this way," Otto told everybody. When Bull saw the huge boulder slam down and close the opening he had just seconds before crawled through. He immediately closed his eyes and started praying to God. And while he thanked the good Lord for many things as he prayed, God sparing his life easily topped the list.

Tab, who had been waiting with everyone else at the bottom of the boulders for Shadow and their three comrades to climb down and join them, was also busy in prayer. Tab thanked God for keeping everyone safe from all the dangers around them. She especially thanked God for protecting Shadow and her big buddy Bull whom she'd grown so attached to and who had just had such a close call.

Soon, the team was back cautiously traveling through the caves tunnel system again. Each member of the team including Shadow kept constantly looking up at the enormous boulders hanging precariously above them. Each wondered if the next one that fell would land on their heads. The one thing that continued to fall was the sweat. It felt like it was over a hundred degrees warmer on this side of the collapsed section of the tunnel than it did on the other. They all assumed correctly that the heat they were experiencing had come from the active volcano.

This was certainly not the cool, almost-borderline cold, trek through the cave that this excursion had started out earlier as it now bordered on brutally hot. As the team walked, each person began simultaneously removing their jackets, caps, and anything else that could help them be cooler. Tab began ripping an old torn T-shirt for rags for everyone to wipe away sweat. As she ripped the last piece and handed it back to her father Roy, to pass on down the line to anyone who wanted one which was everyone, she was suddenly overwhelmed with a sense of immobilizing dread. Tab stopped abruptly and told everyone to do the same.

CHAPTER 39

Mushrooms

"What is it, Tab? What's happening?" her father Roy, asked. "Is it another earthquake?" Chandler asked, looking up at the ceiling of the cave. "No, this is different. I'm not sure yet, but everybody go slow and keep your eyes open. We're getting close to something. So be ready," Tab whispered into her headset radio as she cautiously scanned the tunnel ahead. Tab took no more than ten steps when she came upon the largest batch of mushrooms she had ever encountered. They literally covered the walls and ceiling of the tunnel for the next fifty feet.

Tab, who had her hand on Shadow as she walked, felt the fur on the back of his neck stand straight up. Tab stopped and told everyone to do the same. Tab knew something did not feel right as she looked at all the mushrooms.

"Chandler, step up here please," Tab asked Chandler. Chandler passed Roy and Shadow and came up and stood by Tab. Chandler looked at all the mushrooms, and he could tell something about them had spooked Tab.

"What are they, Tab? Are the mushrooms what's spooking you?" Chandler asked Tab.

"I've never seen anything like them before, and yes something about them has my skin tingling all over," Tab answered Chandler. Chandler waited patiently and watched Tab as she tried to figure out what to do. "It may be this green tint we are looking at them through. I want to see them in regular light. Can we take off our night vision goggles for a few minutes and use our flashlights?" Tab asked Chandler.

"Sure, Tab, no problem. Everybody hear that? Let's go to flashlights, lose the goggles," Chandler told everyone.

As Tab and everyone began to remove their goggles and turn their flashlights on, the cave slowly lit up more and more. What they saw amazed them. The mushrooms were huge, and some had heads as big as softballs. They were dark to royal blue in color, and some stood several inches tall, even drooped over as they were. The most obvious thing about them appeared to be their health. They all looked like they were dying or dead.

Tab took a closer look at a really big one that was closest to her that had grew right out of the cave wall at eye level. And what Tab saw instantly brought out goose bumps on her arms. Tiny-looking little blue boils covered the entire surface of the big blue mushroom identical to the ones she had seen in all her previous lives. Tab immediately felt compelled to get her team and her father out of the area. Hot or not, she did care to test any theories with her friends or her father's lives.

"Everybody, cover your mouth and nose, and let's move through this area as quickly as possible, and nobody touches anything, especially the mushrooms," Tab sternly told everybody. Everyone quickly did as Tab instructed and just used their flashlights to follow her as she took off. Tab told Shadow to trust her, and she threw her jacket over his head and led the big cat and her team through the mushrooms as quickly as she possible.

Tab went a good hundred yards past the mushrooms before Chandler asked her to stop and tell him and everybody what had went on back there. Tab did as Chandler asked her, and as everyone stopped again to have their powwow, Tab took several deep breaths, trying to settle her nerves.

First, Tab looked at her father and then at Chandler "Guys, that was a close one," Tab said, still trying to catch her breath.

"What was a close one, Tab?" her father asked.

"Those mushrooms are the source of the affliction. They are the blue boil disease. They're responsible for what's been killing everyone in northern Angola and in all my stories," Tab told her father and everybody.

"Are we infected now?" Otto asked Tab.

"I don't think we are, but I wanted us out of that area," Tab answered Otto.

"Do you feel how hot it is? Heat seems to stop it from spreading and judging by the looks of those mushrooms back there, I'd say we we're right in thinking it might even kill them," Roy told everyone.

"Wow, that was a close one," Chandler added as he shook his head.

Chandler started to ask Tab another question, but he stopped himself as he looked at her. Tab's eyes were closed, and he could tell she was in deep prayer. Chandler couldn't help himself, and he just stood there and watched her for a moment. An actual angel talking to God Almighty was standing right in front of him. That sight combined with that thought sent chills through every fiber of his being. At that moment, Chandler was filled with contentment he had never known before. He couldn't explain what he felt, but he liked it.

As Tab finished her prayer and opened her eyes, Chandler had forgotten whatever it was he had planned on asking her. Tab wiped away the sweat from her brow and started putting her night vision goggles back on. As the flashlights started going out one by one, everyone put their night vision goggles back on and took their place back behind Tab and Shadow. Through the darkness, the team headed back out—all thankful to have the deadly blue mushrooms far behind them.

Just a short ways up the cave, Tab came to a fork in the tunnel. The path leading left had completely collapsed and was blocked by large boulders.

"I hope that wasn't the way we needed to go," said Otto, pointing toward the collapsed tunnel.

"No, that way led to the other area of the Manduno people or at least it used to," Tab told him.

"Well, at least no one will be sneaking up on us now," Chandler said.

Tab turned right, and the team continued on, now almost two miles deep inside of the cave. Once again, Tab could see a dim light up ahead, and from her perfect memory, Tab knew this was something new. There should not be any other Manduno rooms or entrances in or out of the cave until they reached their destination.

CHAPTER 40

Witch Doctor's Dream

The light got brighter the closer they walked, and soon everyone had to turn off their night vision goggles and remove them. The light was coming from a new long tunnel that led outside to the southern side of the volcano. Chandler thought they should investigate the passage in case it had to be used as an escape route. Soon, the team reached the large opening of this new cave opening.

They walked outside and onto a small over hanging cliff, and as they looked out, they all noticed a big difference. The jungle wasn't as prominent on this side of the mountainous volcano. Fields as well as wooded areas mixed together in what appeared to be more farmland than jungle. A large lagoon could be seen a half mile away nestled next to the volcano with a small creek being fed from out of it. A picturesque water fall fell straight out of the volcano down into the lagoon; it was beautiful sight.

"We have to cross a small river up ahead inside the cave. I never knew where it went or that it came out over here. The Manduno people never leave their jungle for any reason. They will occasionally venture up the volcano a short ways but never over it," Tab told everyone as she starred at the waterfall.

Chandler felt better having found a retreat plan. Everybody else just felt better being outside in the cool air. The temperature outside felt almost cold after being inside the balmy heat of the cave for so long, but no one seemed to mind too much. Even the humidity seemed a lot less on this side of the volcano. Chandler let everyone take a quick break to dry their sweat in the cool breeze.

Anvil and Bull sat next to Tab; Shadow, and Roy on several small boulders outside near the edge of the cliff that faced the lagoon.

"Tab, how do you know this cave so well? Have you spent a lot of time in here exploring them," Bull asked?

"No, actually Bull, I have only been through this cave once before about three hundred years ago. I just have a really good memory," Tab answered Bull.

"Wow, three hundred years ago. Can I ask why you where in the cave way back then, Tab," Bull asked her.

"Sure Bull, if you want to know. I got nothing left to hide anyway. I was born 290 years ago as a Manduno human woman exactly as I was born eighteen years ago in this life. When angels are born into earth as a human being, we normally have no recollection of our heavenly alter egos. We live and die exactly as you guys do. But while we are down here living life, we are constantly learning and going through trials and tribulations that we will one day use in our work with our Lord," Tab told everyone the truth with just a few details purposely left out.

Tab's story had everybody so engrossed that everyone had slowly migrated around her to hear her tell it.

"What work?" Chandler interrupted and asked.

"Counseling, angels are counselors to all of God's creations, among many other things. Messengers and comforters to name a few," Tab answered Chandler. Everyone nodded their heads as Tab confirmed what they had heard their whole lives about the role angels played for God. "As humans, angels have all the same emotions and fears and worries that all humans have. We doubt and we are capable of almost anything while we are down here living life as a human," Tab told them.

"Don't angels have free will up in heaven, Tab?" Bull asked.

"Oh, yes, Bull. Angel's have free will as do all of God's creations. Angels simply love our Heavenly Father God Almighty too much to ever do anything purposely to hurt him or make him think badly of us. Heaven is home to all of the angels, and we are all one big family who love one another very deeply. It would make me sad just to think that one of my brother or sister angels might be hurt or unhappy. God, Jesus, and of all of us angels truly respect and love each other 100 percent to the bottom of our hearts. True, pure love in all of its forms removes the need to ever purposely hurt anyone you care that way about. In fact, just the opposite, love will make you endure great tribulation to ensure those you love are safe and secure. Imagine if everyone on earth just loved one another what a great world this could be."

As Tab said this last statement, everyone gathered around her felt a pinch of human guilt as her words sank in. Tab was right, and they all knew it.

"I'm sorry, Bull. I've been rambling. Back to why I was in the cave so long ago, I was twenty-five years old and a mother of four young children. I must have told this prophecy we're caught up in a thousand times to my children and even to their children's children. I never dreamed it would turn out to be about me, but of course, I did not know I was an angel back then.

"Anyway, all four of my children became deathly ill, so my husband and I took them to our village witch doctor. Our witch doctor said he had never before seen the affliction that was affecting them. He sent us home with a mixture of a few herbs and different plants to try to give to our children, and he told us to give him time to think about what else he needed to do.

"The next morning, the witch doctor sent for my husband and me. He told us that he had dreamed that a cure could be found inside of the volcano—deep in the caves of it's belly. My husband immediately said he would go, but the witch doctor shook his finger at him and forbade it. The witch doctor said in his dream that only I was seen going inside to find the cure, and he was stern when he insisted I was to go alone," Tab said.

"What did you do?" big Bull asked, totally engulfed in her tale.

"I was terrified at the thought of going into the cave alone, but I loved my babies more than I was scared, so I went. Remembering his dream, the witch doctor told me to take seven large torches inside the cave with me. He knew I was scared, so he told me to find courage in the fact that in his dream, he saw me come out bruised but alive. The most exciting thing and the one thing that gave me the most courage was what he told me next. He said when he saw me come out of the cave in his dream that I was carrying the cure. Even had he not told me I would come out alive, I would have still went into the cave to try and save my children.

"As soon as I agreed to go in alone, my husband left to go make the seven large torches we were told I would need. I asked the witch doctor how I would know the cure when I saw it. I remember he paused and waited until my husband had left his hut. As soon as he was sure my husband was gone and could not hear us, he looked right at me and said in a whisper.

"'An eagle man in my dream told me to tell you to look for little yellow berries growing on large root-looking vines that would be growing against and out of the cave walls. That the yellow berries were powerful magic that would cure the affliction that you would need cured.' I never found them until I was on my last torch and was almost all the way through the cave. I was so excited when I found them I picked every single one, and then I rushed as fast as I could to get out of the cave. I came out more than a little bruised, but I was so happy I would be able to save my babies," Tab told everyone.

"Did the berries work when you gave them to your children? Did they save them?" Chandler asked.

"I never even gave the berries to them because by the time I got back out of the cave, all four of my children were as healthy as they could be. It just didn't seem to be a wise move, not knowing anything about the berries and with the witch doctor apparently getting the whole thing wrong. My husband and I just pretended to feed them to our children, and we thanked the witch doctor for all of his doctoring. My kids stayed healthy, and thank God, I died before any of them did," Tab answered Chandler as she shrugged her shoulders.

"Odd, very odd, Tab," Bull spoke out. "That's an odd way for that story to turn out. It sounded for a moment like another angel had helped you back all them years ago," Bull told Tab.

"Turned out that the witch Doctor just made a mistake and that prophecy dream of his was just a simple dream," Tab said of that long-ago witch doctor's dream of her finding the cure.

Chandler told everybody that they needed to get back to business. Everyone felt refreshed and dry, and after everyone got back on their feet and stretched out their legs, they headed back into the cave. As soon as it started getting so dark, they had trouble seeing. They all stopped just long enough to put their night vision goggles back on.

It only took a few moments for the team to get acclimated to viewing everything back through the green-tinted lenses of the night vision goggles as they traveled farther into the darkness of the cave. Soon, the sound of rushing water could be heard, and the more they all continued forward, the louder it became.

CHAPTER 41

Angel Overboard

Finally, Tab had led them all safely to the little river inside of the cave. The very river that they had all seen from the cliff where Tab had told them the story of the last time she had lived as one of the Manduno people. Of course, the river was a magnificent, beautiful waterfall the last time they saw it.

For such a small river, its current moved at rapid speeds. Waves collided against the walls of the cave with such force that the crashing of the water sounded like thunder.

No way could we walk across this river. It would be suicide, Chandler thought. As if Tab had read his mind, she hollered over the noise of the river.

"We can cross up ahead just a little ways farther. There is a natural arch bridge that spans the river or at least there used to be," Tab yelled at the top of her lungs. The path had turned and now paralleled the raging little river. Chandler and Otto looked the river up and down, amazed at the speed it was moving.

The cave suddenly opened up into a giant underground cavern about a football field long. The little river came right out of the wall of the cave at one end and split in two directions. One going down the path we just came from and the other going right back into the wall of the cave at the waterfall end. Luckily, the bridge Tab remembered could be seen still intact and spanning the river. As the team gathered next to the ancient natural arch bridge, every one of them voiced their opinions to the condition and the safety of the bridge.

"Guys, I know this old bridge looks like it's about to fall apart, but it's been here probably for millions of years. It looked just like this back when I crossed it three hundred years ago, and besides, this is the only way across this river," Tab told everyone. Tab had not only heard what they had all said out loud about the bridge, but she clearly heard their thoughts as they worried about crossing it.

"Tab's right, and besides, we ain't about to wade this river," Chandler said, pointing to the giant waves powerfully hitting the cave wall right across from where they all stood.

The river was only about eighteen feet across, and as everyone stared at the bridge, truth be known, it did not appear to be very safe. It looked like it should have been thicker and wider for the distance it spanned. The bridge was only three foot thick and thirty inches wide at its widest point, and it was hard to believe it could even hold its own weight up, let alone the additional weight of a person.

Everyone agreed that only one person at a time should try to cross the bridge. Tab sent Shadow on across, and without hesitation or difficulty, the big cat was up and over the shaky-looking bridge in seconds. Everyone felt so much better when they saw this because they all knew Shadow outweighed anyone of them by four or five times. Roy hated to see his daughter start the climb over the bridge, but he knew she had to.

"Go ahead, baby girl, but please be careful and take your time," her father told her with a worried look on his face. Tab knew how worried her father was, so she leaned up and kissed his cheek and promised she would be careful as she crossed the bridge. Tab started up the bridge just as she had done 290 years ago. Crossing the bridge was more of a balancing act than a stroll across it, and it didn't help any to have the white water rapids splashing and raging below you either. Tab was doing great and had made it halfway when the unexpected happened.

Suddenly, the volcano came alive, and it woke up big and angry. Debris fell from the ceiling, and the entire cave began to shake violently. Even with everything that was falling around them, Roy and the rest of the team kept their eyes on Tab up on the middle of the bridge. Tab appeared to be almost dancing as the tiny bridge swayed back and forth and threw her first one way then another.

Just then, a very loud explosion rocked the mountain, throwing everyone clean off their feet, including Tab. As Tab lost her footing, she fell back and, off the bridge, splashing into the rapids below. Shadow roared, alerting everyone to Tab's dilemma and ran back up on the bridge and watched as Tab helplessly floated down the river. There was little any of the team could do to try and help Tab with the earthquake still throwing them off their feet everytime they tried to stand up. Finally, it eased up enough for everyone to stand up and look for Tab.

Roy had to be restrained by Bull as he tried to jump into the river to try and save his daughter. As everyone headed back down the path following the river, they caught a glimpse of Tab hanging onto some rocks just as her grip slipped, and she was swept under the water and through the wall of the cave. Everyone was in shock and in disbelief as they watched her disappear.

Suddenly, Bull took off running through the cave back in the direction they had all came from.

"Where are you going, Bull?" Chandler asked him through his headset radio.

"She ain't dead. I just know it. I'm headed to that lagoon 'cause if she comes out, that is where she will come out at," Bull told everyone. Roy wiped his eyes and took off after him, and knowing Bull could be right, everyone else did the same thing as Roy, which was to follow Bull.

After Tab felt her grip slip loose from the rock she had been hanging onto, she rolled over in the river just in time to see the wall of the cave rushing at her. Tab's head just nicked the cave wall as the current pulled her down below the surface of the water. Tab immediately took a huge deep breath and held it.

It seemed like forever as the river's current carried her rapidly through the underground world she found herself in. Just as her breath had run out and she thought this must surely be her end, she was blinded by bright light and felt herself falling. Tab landed with a huge splash, thankful to be alive. As she swam to the surface of the water and then somehow to the edge of the lagoon, Tab laid there, too tired to even move.

Tab heard a noise and looked up just as several sharp spears were pointed in her face. She had been through too much to resist, and before she knew it, she had passed completely out, partly from the blow to the head and partly due to sheer exhaustion.

CHAPTER 42

Pygmies

It took the team about twenty minutes to reach the outside entrance they had been at earlier. Shadow had been going crazy since Tab fell into the river. There was only one very steep path that led away from the rocky cliff outside of the cave entrance, but no one even hesitated, and down they all went led by Shadow. The lagoon was only a quick several-minute hike from the cave, and the team made double time of it the whole way.

Everyone openly yelled for Tab as they got close to the lagoon, not caring who heard. Roy fell to his knees when he did not see Tab; he had been so sure she would be here when they arrived. Now Roy feared his precious daughter might be dead, stuck, and drowned inside the underground portion of the river.

"Hey, everybody, come look at this," Otto yelled to everyone. There next to the edge of the lagoon were Tab's night vision goggles and several children-size–looking footprints in the mud.

"She was here. She must be alive," Roy said as tears of joy ran down his face.

"Yeah, but who got her, and where'd they take her?" Chandler asked.

"Looks like a day care found her with all of these little footprints," Anvil said. Bull hit his knees and openly thanked the good Lord for Tab being alive.

"They can't be too far ahead of us, so let's go get her back," Roy told everyone. Nobody had to be told twice on that one, and off they went, following the fresh trail left by her captors.

It only took about forty-five minutes from the lagoon to catch up to Tab and her captors. The team followed the fresh trail right up until they saw smoke from a campfire. The team took cover and stayed out of sight as Chandler broke out his binoculars and got the surprise of his life. Eight little Pigmy warriors were gathered around a campfire, cooking what looked like an old copper pot full of stew.

Chandler could just make out Tab tied up, sitting against an old log. Tab appeared unconscious, and her condition beyond that could not be told.

"It's her, and they have her tied up against an old log," Chandler told everyone. Roy grabbed Chandler's binoculars; he had to see for himself if Tab was okay. As he stared at her through the binoculars, looking for any signs of movement to let him know she was alive and all right, Tab turned to her side and rested her head against the old log. Roy breathed a huge sigh of relief when he saw Tab move.

Bull, who was looking at the pigmys through his own set of binoculars, said something that made everyone stop what they were doing and stare at him. "They're so little they're almost too cute," Bull said out loud. Everyone shook their heads at their big, soft-hearted buddy.

"How are we going to get her back without killing all of them?" asked Anvil seriously.

"Yeah, we're on a mission for God, so I'm guessing he wouldn't appreciate that very much," Bull added.

"Never thought about that, but I guess you're right. They're cooking dinner, so they aren't leaving anytime soon. I guess we got time to come up with a plan," Chandler told everyone.

"We still have to get Tab and Shadow to that hillside before it gets very late, so we can hopefully save the president and all of our friends," Otto reminded everyone.

"I got it. I'll be right back," Bull told everyone as he hurriedly got up and snuck off toward the lagoon. The big cat Shadow knew

Bull had left to go try and find a way to help Tab, so he got up and followed him.

"Got what?" Anvil asked Bull. Bull didn't even take time to answer as he disappeared into the thickets.

"What's he doing?" Chandler asked Anvil. Anvil just shrugged his shoulders unaware as to his comrade's intentions. Bull only walked a short ways before he went over to an odd-looking bush with little purple round berries on it. He dropped to his knees and started digging with his large bowie knife. Shadow came over and, without even knowing why, started helping Bull dig with his big paws.

"That a boy, Shadow, way to go," Bull told Shadow as he dug and dug.

"Maybe we can distract them and then grab her," Roy suggested.

"Maybe we could send Shadow in and scare them off," Anvil thought out loud.

"What if they spear him or worse? Remember, guys, we need him tonight too," Otto reminded everyone. As the team continued trying to come up with a feasible plan, Bull and Shadow crawled back over to them.

"I found some right where Tab said they would be," Bull said excitedly.

"Found what, Bull?" asked Chandler.

"Some of these," he said as he held up five little bulbous onion-looking roots.

"What in the world are they, and why do you have them?" asked Otto.

"They're the nee nee root Tab told us about. She told me where and how to find them," Bull replied.

"Why did she do that?" Anvil asked him.

"Because I asked her, and she told me that's how I know, and it's a good thing to," Bull replied.

"Why what are you going to do with them?" Otto asked.

"Here, let me tell you guys my plan," Bull said as everyone formed a circle, and Bull stretched out his long arms and put them around Roy and Anvil. As big as Bull was, he looked like a pro quarterback in a huddle.

Tab still appeared unconscious or asleep as she sat motionless, leaning against the old log. Four little pygmy warriors stood at the campfire, laughing and talking to the cook. The cook was an ugly little man with a large bullring made of bone pierced right through his nose. He had a total of three very worn-down teeth in his mouth as he chewed what appeared to be chewing tobacco, and as he laughed at the other four little men, he constantly kept spitting juice or something out of his mouth.

The other three little warriors had been out on wood duty apparently because here they all came back with their arms full of branches and sticks, and they dumped it all right beside the campfire. Suddenly, on the opposite end away from the lagoon, Shadow silently walked right into the pygmy camp like he owned the place. Not a single pygmy noticed the huge black panther or even heard him until he had almost gotten all the way to the campfire.

Suddenly, Shadow let out a huge roar that would have made any lion proud. Not only did it jar Tab to consciousness but it also about made the pygmies pee their loincloths. The startled little pygmies screamed and panicked like little girls for just a brief moment when they first saw Shadow in their camp and just how enormous he was. Then they raced to grab their spears.

Shadow slowly back out of their camp then bolted. The race was on as all eight of the little warriors including the one that had been cooking took off screaming after Shadow. Roy, who had been slowly sneaking toward the pygmy's camp, watched all this go down. As the last pygmy ran out of the camp chasing after Shadow, Roy quickly jumped up and ran toward the cooking pot of stew that the pygmies had been cooking. He quickly placed all five nee nee bulbs Bull had found into the stew.

Roy looked over at Tab and saw she was conscious and watching what he had done. Her father held his finger to his mouth, telling her to remain silent. He mouthed he would be back soon to get her, and she slowly nodded okay. Roy wanted so badly to just untie Tab and carry his baby girl out of there and out of danger, but he promised to stick to the plan, so he just turned and ran away as fast as he could.

Just a few minutes later, all eight of the little angry warriors came back into their camp. Tab pretended to still be unconscious as she heard them talk about how Shadow had come into their camp and how lucky he had been to have gotten away. They all grabbed little wooden bowls and started eating their dinner as one after the other took turns telling boastful stories, trying to outdo the previous storyteller. Each story concerned Shadow in some way or another, and each story got more and more outlandish and funny as the nee nee root drug started to kick in.

Tab listened, trying not to laugh, but soon, she couldn't help herself as the words of the little pygmy men started slurring really badly. One storyteller accidentally let out a giant fart as he pranced around acting out how he would have killed Shadow, causing Tab and all the pygmies to bust out laughing. Suddenly, all of the little men started trying to out fart one another, and for some reason, this made Tab and all them laugh even harder. As each of their speech got worse and their farting got longer and louder, this only heightened the pygmies' laughter as they to found it as funny as Tab did.

Suddenly, Tab figured out what her dad had put into their stew and why he hadn't taken her with him when he had the chance. Soon, the pygmies were all in lala land, and the only sound Tab heard was footsteps coming closer to her. Tab looked up to see her father and her whole team walking right at her. Tab was so happy seeing everyone come to her rescue that she cried tears of joy.

Her father untied her and almost choked her he held her so tight. Roy was so happy Tab was alive and okay. He was afraid to let her go, and for the longest time, he just held her tight. Finally, Bull told Roy to give the rest of them a turn, and one by one every member of the team gave her a big hug and voiced their concern for her. Shadow wasn't about to be left out, and he too loved all over Tab. Tab thanked them all for rescuing and saving her life.

Bull and Anvil loosely tied all the pygmies up and carried them closer to their campfire so no predators would try to get at them until the powerful effects of the nee nee drug they had been unwittingly feed wore off. They even threw a few more thick logs into the fire so it would burn longer.

"Is this the way Tracks and the others look right now?" big Bull asked Tab as he pointed to the pygmy's eyes that were rolled back into their heads.

"I'm afraid so Bull, but they'll be okay until we get them back. Just a little while longer, and this will all be over," Tab said, showing the time to Bull on her watch.

CHAPTER 43

Yellow Berries

It was getting late, and everybody knew they were cutting it closer than they wanted to. It was just starting to get dark as they climbed back up to the cave's entrance. Tab and her entire team took one last look back at the picturesque evening view of the lagoon as the sun began to set. Otto handed Tab her night vision goggles back she had accidentally dropped at the lagoon. After quickly putting their night vision goggles back on, the team headed back into the dark cave.

Soon, they had all walked back through the cave and stood at the old bridge once more. This time, Shadow had Tab ride on his back across the bridge. Tab started to dispute the idea, but Shadow pretty much demanded that Tab sit on his back and wrap her arms around his big neck and for her to hold on tight. This time, Shadow and Tab both made it across without any incident. As Tab climbed down from Shadow's back, she hugged his big furry neck and thanked him dearly for helping her across. She rubbed his face and neck as they waited patiently for the rest of the team to make it over the bridge.

After everyone had safely made it over the shaky, old bridge, Tab and Shadow led the team back on their way. Tab told everyone through her headset radio that they should come to the end of the cave in about twenty or thirty minutes. No one minded hearing that news as they were all pretty tired of the cave at this point.

Suddenly, Tab stopped and Chandler was the first to ask her what was wrong. Tab told Chandler nothing was wrong but she wanted to remove her night vision goggles one last time to look for something. Once again, everybody followed Tab's lead and removed their goggles. Tab was the first one to turn on her flashlight. Tab shined it up and down the cave walls in search of something, and soon everyone was shining their flashlights all around the cave.

"What are we looking for, Tab?" her father asked her.

"Do you guys remember my story that had the little yellow berries in it? Well, around this area is where I found them, and I was just curious if they still grew in this area for some reason," Tab told her father.

"Down here, I think I found some of them," Bull said excitedly.

Sure enough, a whole batch of the little yellow berries were growing off large vines growing out of the cave walls just like Tab had said they did in her story.

"Are we taking some of these berries with us for some reason?" Chandler asked Tab.

"No, I was just curious if they were still here, that's all," Tab replied. "Let's go, guys I'm sorry I had us stop," Tab said as she started putting her night vision goggles back on. Everyone did the same, and as the flashlights slowly started going out, everyone once again found themselves in the green-tinted world of the night vision goggles.

The drums and chanting started to once again be heard as Tab and her team left the little yellow berry vines behind. Chandler couldn't help it, but he found himself thinking about the yellow berries and how much money a pharmaceutical company might pay to have access to them. Chandler decided to add them to his list of "come and gets" if he ever made it out of all this alive. He had quite an impressive list put together too with the seven gold disc and the cache of rare gems and rubies in the throne chair.

As the team neared the end of the cave, the drums and chanting had become almost deafening as they echoed off the cave walls. The entire Manduno village was in high gear down below, celebrating their gifts to Mantoro, their volcano god. Finally, Tab and Shadow led the team to the end of the cave. Everyone cautiously peeked outside and stood at the entrance, now almost freezing. The unusually cool temperature outside hadn't went away.

Every star in the sky could be seen overhead as there wasn't a cloud in the night sky. The moon was full and hung over the volcano like a huge street light. The moon was so bright you could have read by it. Everyone started getting their jackets back out and putting them on along with anything else they could find to put on to keep warm. Roy walked up to Tab who had her jacket in her lap doing something to it.

"What are you doing, baby girl?" her father asked. Tab had a white chalky rock and was writing on her jacket.

"This," Tab said as she held up her jacket to show her father. Tab had wrote _Tab_ across the top left breast of her jacket. "I just got to thinking that the water witch somehow saw my name written on my clothing somewhere, and here I am out in this jungle with nothing with my name on it. So I thought I'd fix that problem and give the water witch a way to see it," Tab told her father.

"Well, isn't that thoughtful. I raise such good kids I should have had more," her father joked with her.

"Yeah, but you only need one when she's an angel," big Bull added.

"Oh, Bull, you're so sweet," Tab told her big old buddy.

"So, Tab, when will all of this start?" Chandler curiously asked.

"I'd say soon, maybe an hour or so from the sound of the drums," Tab answered.

Suddenly, the old volcano let loose with several small explosions, once again throwing most of the team off their feet. The volcano shook so violently Tab and her team ran out of the cave, and to their shock and amazement, red molten lava steadily flowed out from the top of the volcano. Two huge rivers of bright red lava flowed down the volcano on the other side of the village where they had all just came from.

The entrance to the cave that they all were hidden in earlier this morning was now covered completely by one of the rivers of lava. The lava quickly made it to the jungle where it ignited everything it touched, and soon vast parts of the jungle was on fire. The lava finally reached the river where it turned to steam upon impact. The sound of the steam hissing as it was sent into the air just added to the ferocious atmosphere.

Through all this, the drums and chanting never even slowed down. For the next hour, the volcano never let up, and everyone was so engrossed by the eruption that no one even noticed Chandler had disappeared. Roy put his arm around Tab's shoulders as they watched all the excitement. Roy knew that soon Tab would be on her own to face whatever laid ahead.

Finally, the volcano quit as quickly as it had begun, but the jungle unfortunately was still furiously on fire.

"Will this stop or postpone anything?" Otto asked Tab.

"Actually, just the opposite, the eruptions is why they're doing all of this to begin with. They honestly believe that sacrificing all of these men tonight will make the eruptions quit and go away," Tab replied to Otto.

Her father Roy, was getting more and more worried as the time went by. "You ready for this?" her father asked, wishing he could take her place somehow.

CHAPTER 44

Wings

"You know Dad, I am finally ready. Back home in my bedroom when God showed me who I really was, I had never ever been alone up to that point in my entire existence, not even for a second. And, Dad, I have been around for a really, really long time. So as you could imagine, I've been a little lost and even scared at times. I even had my faith tested a few times.

"So I guess I needed this little adventure to prove not to my Heavenly Father God that I would and could do his will away from him but to myself. Because, of course, he already knew I could. I had to learn to be decisive and to act on his behalf on faith as all of his other creations have to do. I had to learn the hard way that he has my back even when he isn't holding my hand. Yes, Dad, I am ready. I know God is here with me because God is everywhere," Tab said with clarity and resolve.

Just then, the drums abruptly quit, and everybody looked at each other.

"It's time to go," Tab told everyone as Shadow walked over to Tab and knelt down so she could climb onto his back. As Shadow rose back up onto all fours, it truly was a majestic sight seeing Tab sitting up on his back.

"What do we do?" asked Otto.

"Just watch from the cave. You'll know when to come down," Tab replied. Tab took one more look at her father, Roy. "I love you.

You've been such a great father. Please tell Mom I love her," Tab told her father.

"You tell her yourself, Tab. You are coming back, aren't you?" her father asked with a worried look on his face.

"I honestly don't know how this will all play out. Thy will be done," Tab said softly as a big tear rolled down her face.

"Tell God we need you here," her father pleaded as Tab and Shadow turned and slowly walked down the hillside. Bull came over to Roy as he stood there and watched Tab ride off. He knew Roy was hurting at the thought of Tab leaving this world to go be with their Heavenly Father God Almighty because his big heart was breaking too. Bull put his big arm around his little buddy just as Roy broke down. Hearing her father make that last statement nearly broke her heart. But Tab had to put those thoughts out of her mind; she had a mission to complete and an A to get.

Tab wiped her eyes one more time, and then her face turned from sad to one of complete concentration. Just below her, she could hear the executioner loudly making his boastful speech to Mantoro, their false god of the volcano. As Tab and Shadow silently moved into view of the sacrificial arena, she could see Watson laid out on top of an ancient-looking, bloodstained wooden table waiting for the executioner's axe. Everyone was watching the executioner as both Tab and Shadow waited for their cue. As soon as the executioner finished talking, Tab and Shadow watched as he slowly raised his broad head axe high above his head. Watson had just seconds to live as the executioner paused to take aim.

Just then, Shadow let out the loudest roar ever. Everyone, everywhere, stopped what they were doing and looked toward the hillside where Tab sat majestically upon the back of Shadow. Silence fell across the huge crowd of villagers as everyone realized what this was, and they all stood motionless and afraid. Her father Roy, and the rest of her team, including Chandler who had just came out of the cave, all stood and watched silently, each praying to God for him to help Tab in any way he could.

Tab closed her eyes for the briefest of time, and when she opened them, God was in them. Tab seemed to slightly lean forward and then sat straight up as two of the most beautiful, angelic, and extremely large solid white angel wings rose up and out from her back. Tab's wingspan stretched out six feet in each direction. The glow from all the lit torches and forest fires turned the underside of Tab's wings almost golden looking. Every single Manduno man, woman, and child, fell to their knees and bowed their heads. Tab's own team behind her each stood in awe at the heavenly and majestic vision before them. Roy had never been so happy and proud of his daughter. He wished his wife, Christina, could have been here to have witnessed their daughter, Tab, in all her heavenly splendor.

Suddenly, Tab spoke to the Manduno people, but amazingly, somehow even her team could understand her words.

"A very deadly affliction has come into your village, and even as I speak to you, it is relentlessly spreading throughout your land and to everyone of you and your children. The one true God has sent me here to help you and your people survive this affliction. Please release my friends and their king and care to their needs as they are also friends of the One True God."

As Tab spoke, she brought her beautiful wings down and folded them against her back. Chandler and her entire team slowly walked down and stood behind her as she continued talking to the Manduno people. "Behind me you see eight more friends who will come into your village to help you attend to your sick and needy. Treat them all with respect and allow no one or nothing to hurt them as they are here to help you.

"I will wish to speak to your king and his high council as soon as they can assemble. Now, everyone, please go home and be with your loved ones so that death may pass you by." Tab looked out over the villagers and saw one royal-looking Manduno man slowly stand and look up at her. By his attire, Tab knew he was the Manduno king before he even spoke.

"Your coming was foretold ages ago, and as king, I speak for all of the Manduno people when I say thank you. We will all do as you have instructed," the king stood proudly and said.

"Thank you, King Jacobi, I can tell you are a brave and great ruler of your people," Tab told the king, who was surprised the eagle lady knew his name.

"What should my people call you, great winged one?" the king humbly asked.

"I am Tab the angel, and I am a servant and herald to the One True God," Tab told the king as he bowed his head in respect then turned and walked away to make sure his people and his counsel did as Tab the angel had asked.

Down below, everyone was busy doing as Tab had instructed. The villagers slowly dispersed and headed home to their huts. The Manduno warriors and the executioner untied all the men and the president and led them back into the cave and into the holding cell next to the sacrificial arena so they would be safe.

"Your wings are awesome, Tab. Can I touch them?" Bull asked as he was reaching toward them.

"Sure, Bull, you can't hurt them," Tab told him.

"I guess you got that A you were so worried about getting, baby girl," her father joked with her.

"Not yet, Dad," Tab told him, looking a little concerned.

"Why not, Tab? You stopped our men from being executed and you saved the president. Isn't that all you had to do?" Chandler asked.

"No one is saved yet. The blue boil disease is still here, and I've yet to be shown how to deal with it. Somehow I've missed something," Tab told her team.

CHAPTER 45

The Cure

"That's odd, Tab. I would have thought that God would have just healed everyone," Bull commented.

"What did you say, Bull?" Tab asked?

"I said it's odd that—" Bull was interrupted by Tab before he can even finish his statement.

"That's what I thought you said," Tab said excitedly. Everyone could tell Tab had just figured something out from what Bull had said. "Bull, you may have just saved all of us. But I have to hurry. I don't think Mr. Watson has much time left," Tab said with a worried look on her face.

"Hurry and get what, Tab?" her father Roy, asked.

"The little yellow berries, Dad. Remember the dream the witch doctor told me when I was a twenty-five-year old Manduno mother of four, how a winged man in his dream told him to tell me I would need the little yellow berries for the cure I needed? Well, they were never intended for my children back then. I see that now. I was only sent into the cave back then to learn my way around it. Those berries were meant for me to use now in this life. I've got to hurry and go get every single one of them. Everyone will need to eat one," Tab told everyone.

"I hope this is enough. I grabbed everyone I could find," Chandler said as he took a large duffle bag from around his shoulder and handed it to Tab.

"What, why do you have these, Chandler?" Tab asked as she looked into the bag.

"To save the day apparently," Chandler quickly thought and said. Tab looked at him knowingly then smiled.

"Thy shall not lie, but thank you, Chandler. You may have just saved the day," Tab said as Chandler smiled and nodded his head.

"If there isn't enough for everyone to have one of their own, which I don't think there is, we could 'Pull a Bull,' Tab," Chandler suggested.

"What's 'Pull a Bull' mean, Chandler," asked Bull.

"We'll mix them with water like lemonade to make them go farther. Then we can just give everyone a shot of the cure, kind of like you did putting the nee nee root in the pygmies beef stew," Chandler told Bull and everybody. Bull smiled as Chandler explained his statement of we could "Pull a Bull."

"Wow, great idea, Chandler. Thanks to all of you. I may just get that A after all," Tab gratefully told everyone. "But let's not forget our Heavenly Father. To God goes the glory because without him, we could not have succeeded in our mission. He helped us in so many ways, starting centuries ago with the prophecies and the dreams of the Manduno witch doctors to light the path and guide us. He brought this team together and even gave us Shadow to protect and help us. There is no doubt in my mind God Almighty should get this game ball. Now thanks to him we all will survive this deadly blue boil disease," Tab said as everyone bowed their heads and silently thanked the Lord.

Anvil broke the silence, "Bull and me will start mixing several containers of Tab's yellow berry cure aid. Then we can all split up and start taking it around to everyone," Anvil said.

"Yeah, maybe we can even get the Manduno people to help us so we don't miss anyone," Chandler suggested.

"Great, guys, thank you so much, but before you start, can you please go ahead and give Mr. Watson his own berry to eat? I can sense he hasn't got much time left as he is very bad off. Now I've got to go meet with the Manduno King and his high council and attend to my Heavenly Father's business," Tab told everyone.

"If you have to leave afterwards, please stop and say good-bye and maybe give your old dad a hug," Tab's father said with a tearful look.

"I'm sure that shouldn't be a problem, Dad, so don't worry," Tab reassured him.

Tab stayed atop Shadow as they went down the hillside to the village below. Maybe it was for grand effect, or maybe Tab just liked it. Her team wasn't sure which one it was, but it was still a very majestic vision to witness. When Tab and Shadow reached the bottom of the hillside getting ready to enter the village, something caught Tab's eye and made her turn her head.

CHAPTER 46

A Prophet Honored

There standing twenty feet from her was the ghostly transparent image of the water witch. Tab had Shadow stop, and the two looked at each other for the longest time. The water witch was a short, older-looking Manduno woman with wild, messy gray hair. She had a large wooden walking stick in one hand and several eagle feathers in the other. Her eyes where sky blue, which was strange to Tab as almost all the Manduno people's eyes were brown. Tab thought they were beautiful.

Finally, Tab smiled at her and mouthed the words *thank you* to the water witch who seemed very surprised that Tab could see her. The water witch smiled back at Tab and bowed her head in respect and then slowly disappeared. Tab briefly wondered why the water witch had kept this encounter between the two of them out of her prophecy. In all the many times she had ever heard it told, not once was it ever mentioned.

Unknown to everyone except the water witch, the actual reason she kept the meeting out of the prophecy was because she felt so honored—not only did the eagle lady see her in her vision, but she actually smiled at her and thanked her. Maybe it was a selfish act to keep this part of her vision only to herself, but it was such a treasured moment for the water witch that she felt it should stay just between the eagle lady and herself forever. The water witch was old and wise enough to have learned that everything did not have to be told.

By the time Tab and Shadow finished the Lord's work with the Manduno king and his high council, it was almost midnight. Tab could feel how exhausted Shadow was under her, so she had him stop, and she slid down from his back and walked beside him. As the two got to the stone stairs that pyramided up and made the sacrificial arena, Tab leaned over and gave Shadow the biggest hug ever. Tab put both her small arms around the big furry neck of Shadow and thanked him from the bottom of her heart for all he had done for not only her and her friends but also for her Heavenly Father God.

Tab sent Shadow on ahead and told him to go get some sleep, and she would see him in the morning. Shadow did not want to leave Tab, but reluctantly, he too did as she asked him. Tab watched Shadow lumber off up the stone stairs to go be with her father and everybody else at the holding cell at the top of the sacrificial arena. Tab wanted to just take a moment alone and let everything that had went on tonight sink in.

The meeting with the king and his high council had went great. The Manduno people were so appreciative that they easily agreed to accept her Heavenly Father God as their one and only deity. Tab told the king and the high council she would send a team of missionaries of the One True God to come into their village and teach them about him and his teachings. Tab talked in great detail of God and of his love.

Tab told them about the One True God's son, Jesus Christ, and of his sacrifice on the cross and how they never needed to ever harm anybody else as his sacrifice was all that would ever be needed from here on out—that to accept the One True God's son, Jesus Christ, as their personal Savior and accept that he died for their sins was a promise to salvation and to everlasting life. Tab felt so happy thinking about how the Manduno people had accepted both her Heavenly Father God and his Son, Jesus Christ. Tab felt honored in succeeding with her mission to save the president and how everything else had turned out.

Tab then felt something she had waited to feel since waking up from that nap on the night of her birthday.

CHAPTER 47

God

Tab felt her inner connection to God. She was so happy, and excited that for a minute or two, she just stood there, overwhelmed with joy. Her large, beautiful wings wrapped around her like friends giving her a hug.

Suddenly, Tab realized that seeing her Heavenly Father God Almighty was but a thought away. Tab closed her eyes and whispered out loud the same little prayer she always said before she traveled using the Holy Spirit. In a blink of the eye, Tab disappeared from the Manduno village and instantly reappeared in heaven in the throne room of God Almighty. Before she even opened her eyes, she knew two things. One, she was back home in heaven, and two, she was standing in the presence of her Heavenly Father, God Almighty himself.

The only thing better than being back home in heaven was standing right in front of her. God opened his arms and welcomed Tab back home like a daughter who had been off at college. Tab hugged him tighter than she could ever remember hugging him. Tab looked up at her Heavenly Father.

"Finally, Father, we are together. Please never leave me again. I have missed you so much," Tab said as she cried tears of joy in the arms of her Heavenly Father.

"Tab, listen to what you're saying. Why you know I would never leave you? There wasn't one second that I wasn't standing right by your side the entire time you thought you were alone. And another thing, Tab that I want you to know is I have never been more proud of you. Tab, someday you're going to make an excellent angel up here in heaven," her Heavenly Father told her. Tab heard the word *someday*, and her heart sunk. "What's wrong, Tab," God asked Tab knowingly.

"Nothing is wrong, Father. I guess I just got ahead of myself. I thought maybe I had graduated and that I was a full-fledged working-class angel for you. I guess I just got excited—that's all—but I'm okay," Tab said, a little brokenhearted.

"Tab, you did graduate, and you are a full-fledged working-class angel," God told her smiling. "I just thought you might want to go back to earth and finish your life with Roy and Christina until I call you home. I know how much you three love each other and the universe needs that kind of love. There is one condition though that you will have to agree to first," God told Tab.

"Anything, oh Father, thank you so much. You are the best. May I ask what the condition is my father?" Tab excitedly asked God.

"Just like your earthly father Roy feared, Chandler on the request of his boss, the president of The United States, is going to offer you a job, and I want you to accept the position," God said.

"Of course, Father, thy will be done. May I ask why you want me to take the job?" Tab asked.

"Of course, you may, Tab. Your little adventure down on earth turned out so well that I thought why end it now. The earth is full of situations I planned on fixing someday, and someday is here. You will be the vessel I will use to fix them, if that's okay with you, Tab. I'm sure they will let you keep your same team together if you ask them," God said with a big smile. Tab didn't even have to think about her answer and said yes immediately. "You know I'll have to have those wings back until you come back home to stay. And will you be okay not seeing me until you get back?" God asked Tab?

"That's the part that's hardest of all, but yes, I will be okay. It took a little while, but I know what to do while we're apart now," Tab reassured him.

"What's that, Tab?" God asked, wanting to hear Tab say it.

"Use my faith, dear Father," Tab told him.

"If I remember yours is the size of a mountain, isn't it?" God smiled and said. Tab tried to say "bigger," but before she could get the words out of her mouth, she was back standing at the stone stairs that led up to the sacrificial arena.

Once again, Tab could feel the inner connection she normally had with her Heavenly Father was gone. She wasn't scared this time though nor did she feel alone. Tab knew he was right beside her, and this made her feel safe and loved. It was then that Tab noticed she still had her angel wings, but Tab knew they wouldn't last. Why she still had them or how long she would keep them Tab just didn't know. Maybe God would let her keep her wings until her work was totally finished, and she left the jungle, Tab thought. Tab knew only God had the answers to all those questions.

CHAPTER 48

A Father's Love

Tab walked up the pyramiding stone staircase and saw across the small arena that everyone except her father Roy appeared to be inside the large cave that The Manduno executioner kept his holding cell in. It had been several hours since Tab had left her team to go meet with The King and his high council. As Tab walked into the well-lit up cave, she saw Tracks, the captain, his four other men, and even Mr. Watson all sitting up and looking very hungover. The nee nee root was a powerful drug, but it looked like they were all finally coming down from its toxic side effects. The president, who had never been drugged with the nee nee root nor even treated badly, was standing next to Chandler and her team, talking with them.

As Tab walked up, she was met with a king's welcome. Everyone hugged her and told her how worried they had all been about her and about maybe not getting to see her ever again. Just as Tab started to ask about her father's whereabouts, the president interrupted her before she could ask.

"Young lady, I have heard so much about you and about everything you and these brave men went through to rescue me, and I want to thank you for saving my life," the president told Tab, and she could feel how sincerely he meant what he said. "May I ask you a couple of questions," the president asked Tab.

"Yes sir, Mr. President," Tab replied.

"What's it like being an angel for God and is heaven as good as they say it is?" he asked.

"It's like having the best job in the universe with the best boss ever. And to answer your last question, Mr. President, heaven is heaven," Tab happily answered him.

The president, being a very religious man, smiled when he heard Tab's answers. "Thank you again from the bottom of my heart for saving my life," he told Tab.

"You're welcome, Mr. President, but like I keep saying all the glory goes to God Almighty. We were just a willing vessel he used to do his bidding. But truthfully, you're such a good moral man. It was a pleasure coming to your aid. If you really want to thank me, then just keep doing what you do and keep up the good fight," Tab told the president.

"Thank you for those kind words, Tab. I will," the president once again said.

"Tab, he wants to do more than just keep up the good fight. He's asked me to offer you a job, believe it or not. Told me you could keep this same team together including me," Chandler told Tab, not thinking for a minute an actual angel would say yes and accept an offer to work for the CIA.

"I accept," Tab said. "But I may be a little picky as to the missions I agree to go on," Tab told a very shocked Chandler. The president and all her team were so surprised and happy that Tab had accepted Chandler's offer that they literally shouted with joy.

"Mr. President, you will need to go on the hunt for these very special little yellow," Tab said as the president interrupted her.

"Berries," he said as he finished her statement. "Chandler has already filled me in about the cure, Tab. Thank you so much. I will get people on it as soon as we get back," he gratefully told her.

"You're welcome, sir, and it has been such a pleasure finally getting to meet you. I've got to go find my father, if you will excuse me, Mr. President," Tab said as she excused herself.

"Certainly Tab, it was nice meeting you to, and I look forward to working with you," said the president as Tab walked off in search of her father.

Tab went over to Bull and asked him if he knew where her father had run off to. Bull told her that even though most of the women of the Manduno tribe had taken over giving out the "curade" to everyone in the village and around it that her father Roy, even as exhausted as he was, continued helping and refused to quit. Tab immediately went to look for him.

Shadow, who had awakened when Tab first came in, ran to her side to go with her. Tab asked Shadow to use his keen sense of smell to find her father. Like a giant black bloodhound, Shadow put his big nose to the ground and took off in search of Roy as Tab followed close behind him. Roy had apparently been to a lot of huts, helping families of the Manduno people as Shadow led Tab to one hut after the other as he followed Roy's scent.

Finally, up several huts away, Tab caught a glimpse of her father and a Manduno woman as they walked into yet another hut. As Tab and Shadow got closer to the hut, Tab heard the Manduno woman waking up the family and telling them they had to drink this special medicine from the angel so they would live. What amazed Tab was what her father started saying. Tab knew that her father knew that the Manduno people inside the hut could not possibly understand him. But there he was talking as if they could.

Tab stood outside the hut and listened to her father.

"Did you guys see my daughter, the angel? Wasn't she the greatest? Do you all know that she will probably have to leave when she is done here? That will break her mother's heart and mine too. So I am going to stay up all night and help save as many of you good people as I can in the hopes that God will see how hard I am working and maybe answer my prayers and let my baby girl come back and stay with us. We love her so much, and we need her so badly—she's our world," Roy said.

He was so exhausted and emotional he started to break down and cry. Tab couldn't stand to hear her father in such heartbreak, and when she heard him start to cry, she started tearing up too.

"Knock, knock, is anybody home?" Tab loudly said, wiping away a large tear from her eye as she stood outside the huts bamboo door. Roy knew that voice and immediately went to the door and opened it. Like an answer to his prayers, there stood his beautiful daughter, Tab, standing with Shadow. Both Tab and Roy broke down as they held each other.

"Dad, you're breaking my heart. Quit being so sad," Tab tearfully told her father. Tab couldn't stand to see her mother or her father cry or even be upset without crying herself.

"Oh, Tab, I thought I would never see you again when you never came back. I didn't know how I was going to tell your mother, Christina, that you were gone. I didn't know what was happening, and my hearts been so broken," her father told her, still crying. Tab hugged him so tight, still crying herself.

"Dad, I've got some bad news, and you're not going to like it when I tell you," Tab told her father, preparing him for the news.

"I already know what you're going to say. You have to leave—don't you?—and you'll probably never get to come back," her father said with his heart breaking.

"No, Dad. That's not even close to the bad news I've got to tell you," Tab told her father.

"What is it then, Tab? Tell me the bad news," her father pleaded.

"The president had Chandler offer me a job just like you feared, and I accepted it," Tab smiled and told her father. Even though the words came out of her mouth, her father, Roy, was still too heartbroken, thinking about losing his only daughter, for the words to register.

"How are you going to go away to do God's work and accepted a job here with Chandler, which, by the way, I told you he would offer you a job. Help me catch up, baby girl. You're losing me here," her father said with a very bewildered look on his face.

"Well, I am going to be doing God's work, but instead of going away and doing it, God asked me to do it here on earth so I could stay close to you and mom," Tab told her father with a big smile on her face. This time, her words started sinking in, and with a big smile, he looked Tab right in the eyes.

"Really, Tab, you can stay with us?" her father asked with a happy heart.

"I sure can Dad, but remember I have to work with the CIA as a condition of my staying down here," Tab reminded him.

"As long as you and Chandler understand that we're a package deal," her father said sternly.

"I guessed as much," Tab replied.

Roy hugged Tab really hard and then thought for a moment and laughed. "My daughter, The CIAngel."

T H E   E N D

ABOUT THE AUTHOR

Roy M. Dawes born in 1965 in Lexington, KY. Shortly after that my family and I moved to Anderson, IN. where I went to school from Kindergarten through twelfth grade. Graduating midterm so I could go to work with a local electrical contractor. The following year I joined The IBEW and have worked as an IBEW electrician ever since. I love my Union. At age 25 I moved back to my beloved state of KY. Where I have resided pretty much ever since.

This is my first attempt at writing a book. It was a roller coaster of highs and lows and a lot of work but now that it is done I am finding it more and more rewarding as I look forward to readers hopefully liking it and maybe even being touched by it. I have always been fascinated with The Bible and its stories and especially, Angels. This is just a made up story so please take it as such. I hope you enjoy reading it. Thank you, Roy Dawes